HIS LUCKY BRIDE

THE MAIL ORDER BRIDES OF GRAY ROCK

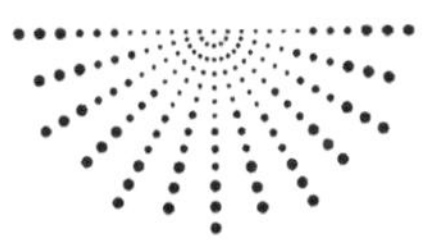

INDIANA WAKE

SWEETBOOKHUB.COM

WELCOME TO GRAY ROCK

Welcome to this series of western historical romances. This is a new series that I have been working on for some time and I can't wait to share the books with you.

All of them are a complete romance and a full story. They are also sweet and clean with no nasty surprises.

Carrie McCord was worried about her son. He had a good job and is a lovely man but there were no women in the mining town and Jamison didn't seem to be interested in finding a wife.

Hoping for grandchildren before she was too old to enjoy them, Carrie took things into her own hands and sent off for a mail order bride. Read all about it in The Miner's Courageous Bride.

Now that her son is married, other miners are looking for brides. Can Carrie work her magic once more?

* * *

Also available: Safe In His Arms

Find out about new releases, get special offers, and receive 3 free books by joining my <u>exclusive newsletter</u>

CHAPTER ONE

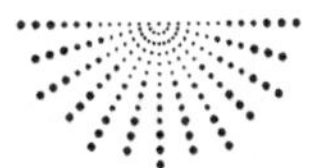

eter Quinn shut his eyes and smiled as the cool air hit his skin. It was really hot out that day. The sun's rays were harsher than usual. It made it even worse that he had to work in the mine on such a day. Peter would much rather find a lake and have a nice swim.

"Goodness, it is hot."

Peter slowly opened his eyes and smiled at Jamison who had come to sit at his side. "I was just thinking the same thing."

It had been months since Eugene's wedding. Peter would be lying to himself if he claimed their marriage hadn't affected their friendship somehow. Jamison and

Eugene barely had time for him now. Not that Peter was complaining. His close friends now had families to take care of, and Peter always made sure to be present when needed.

There was an obvious upside to Jamison and Eugene's new status. Peter had come to realize just how much he loved children. He was aware of the fact that he craved a big family, but seeing how excited he got when he visited Jamison's home, and got to help them build the crib, Peter was certain of it now. It brought him so much joy to be part of the whole process. Though at first, he had been annoyed when Gloria chose Eugene, he now knew that it had been the best thing to happen. Though he would have cared for her, he would never have had the life he so wanted.

But it didn't make up for the fact that he was lonely. After Drusilla and Gloria arrived, Gray Rock had begun to feel like a family. Everyone cared about one another. There were no lines or secrets between them. They would meet almost every day... mostly for dinner and talk about work, Drusilla's pregnancy, or anything that was a topic of interest. Anyone who saw them could not imagine that Peter went home every night, and wouldn't stop sighing. He was lonely, he didn't feel complete.

"What are you thinking about?" Jamison asked, jabbing Peter on the arm. "You're always thinking a lot these days."

Peter scoffed. "Like you don't know why I'm so quiet, Jamie."

"I have an idea, but I'd like to hear it from you first," Jamison told him. "Talk to me, Peter. What is on your mind?"

"Not much," Peter answered and sighed. "But the one thing on my mind feels like a ton. I have a headache."

"Well, I reckon that isn't unusual given that you work in a mine," Jamison said. "But come on, Peter. Let's hear it."

Peter glanced at him and turned to stare blankly at the rolling land over the river. "Would it be weird to say that I'm lonely?"

Jamison raised his eyebrows and paused. "Well, I think I can understand why you would be lonely. But you know it's not for long, right? And you know you have us... right?"

"It's not that," Peter said and adjusted where he sat. "I love everything going on in my life right now. I love being around you, Drusilla, Eugene, and Gloria. I love helping you build the crib even though you make so many mistakes and frustrate my efforts." He stopped to chuckle at his friend. "I love the late-night dinner we always have where we talk about the most trivial things and laugh. I love Steven and his hundred questions per day. I mean, I love everything. But it's just…"

"There's still a void?" Jamison asked.

"Something like that," Peter answered. "I still want a family of my own. It feels like it's taking forever. I don't know… the more I stay home alone, the more time I have to think. I mean, I really want to get married as soon as possible, but what if it doesn't work out, what if something goes wrong like the last time? What if I try, and fail again? What if I never even find love? What if the next woman that shows interest in me turns out to be very different from me? What if…"

"Peter," Jamison called him and chuckled. "Stop with the worrying, would you? I understand where you're coming from, but you shouldn't let thoughts like that make you feel this way.

"It's not my fault for thinking I'm unlucky in life given how things ended the last time," Peter said. "I don't want to just marry, Jamison. I want to…"

"Fall in love?" Jamison asked.

"Yes. I want to experience love," Peter said. "I thought I would have that with Gloria, but that didn't happen, and it makes me wonder if it will happen at all. Will I just marry for convenience? Or will I find the woman that will finally capture my heart?"

Jamison placed a hand on Peter's shoulder. "Just trust my mother like you always have. You said it yourself; at first, you thought Gloria was the one, but it didn't work out only because you have different interests. Mother didn't get it right, and she admitted to this fact. Now, she spends her days going through newspapers, trying to get it right this time. Trust her."

"I trust her, Jamie," Peter said. "But there is a limit to what Carrie can do for me. She can only find me a match. It's up to me and that match to make it work. What if..."

"Peter, I don't want to hear the words 'what if' come out of your mouth again," Jamison told him. "Stop. Just keep an open mind and trust that things will happen exactly how you want them to. Being negative won't bring you any luck. It's much better to say good things than think bad things."

Peter turned to Jamison. "You really think I should still be hopeful?"

"I really do. It's not over yet," Jamison said. "In fact, it's just the beginning for you. Peter, you have no idea how excited we are to see how things turn out for you. We are all here to cheer you on and help in every way possible. I know more than anyone that you deserve to be happy. You take good care of others. It's only fair that good things happen to you."

Peter shook his head. "Good things don't always happen to good people."

"Now, what did we just talk about?" Jamison asked. "Don't think like that. Come on, say what you really want out loud."

Peter bit his lower lip, a reaction borne from his hesitancy. "Well, I want someone that gets me. I would really not want to settle. I wouldn't want my bride to settle for me either. I don't know... I just want to know what love feels like, Jamison. Is that too much to ask?"

"No." Jamison chuckled. "It's not too much at all. If you want, I can tell you in detail what it feels like. You know I've had the opportunity to experience it myself."

Peter laughed and shoved Jamison playfully. "No, thank you."

Deep down, Peter knew Jamison was right. Thinking negative thoughts wasn't helping his situation at all. In fact, it was making it worse. It was much better to be hopeful that sooner or later, he would find his bride.

CHAPTER TWO

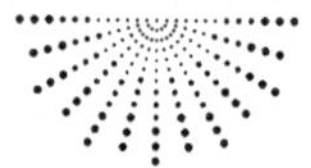

Carrie stood by the fence with a newspaper shoved underneath her arm. She had just said hello to Gwen, the florist at the market, and decided to remain by the wooden fence. There was no one at home she could talk to. Jamison had gone to work, and Drusilla was asleep in her room. The baby bump had already started to show, and Drusilla was starting to get tired very easily. Carrie always asked her to rest, but Drusilla preferred moving around. She always found it difficult to lie down during the day. She was always so restless.

Seeing Drusilla sleep so soundly put Carrie at ease. The idea that Carrie was going to have her first grandchild excited her so much that she refused to leave Drusilla's side. There were times when they would stay up for most of the night, talking about how Carrie birthed Jamison. Carrie made sure to tell Drusilla all the tips she knew, things she had to eat, how to sleep... it wasn't easy, but they were getting by. Carrie was thrilled that soon, the cries and giggles of a child would fill their home.

"Carrie, what are doing by the fence?"

Carrie shook her head softly, snapping out of her thoughts. She turned to her left and found Becky standing by her own fence with a bucket in her hand and a pile of clothes on her shoulder. Becky Montgomery was Carrie's next-door neighbor. She was a plump, red-haired cheerful woman who had a tiny voice. Becky always wanted to know what was going on around her.

"You're with a newspaper, again?" Becky asked, leaning on the fence. "For months, I've always seen you with the paper. It seems you've taken a liking to reading them."

"Good afternoon, Becky," Carrie greeted. "How are you today?"

Becky shrugged her shoulders. "Fine. But I could be better. How are you, and how is Drusilla? I see her baby bump is getting bigger by the day."

"She's fine, thank you for asking," Carrie answered. "She found it hard to sleep all night, so she is taking a rest now."

Becky nodded and sighed. "I recall when I was pregnant. I could sleep all day long. There was this one time when I was pregnant that I woke up in the morning, had my breakfast, and went back to bed, only to wake up the next day. I was so heavy during that period."

"Ah, well, it was different for me," Carrie said. "My belly didn't show for months. In fact, I barely had any symptoms until about five months in. Then it all came at once, and I was miserable."

"Tell me about it," Becky said. She diverted her gaze to the newspaper and nudged her head. "But really, Carrie. Why do you always have a newspaper with you?"

Carrie placed the newspaper in her palm and sighed. "Do you know Peter Quinn?

Becky nodded. "Of course."

"Well, I'm trying to find a bride for him. He told me about his interest to settle down and start a big family and I really want to help him achieve this. So, whenever I can, I go through the newspapers to find adverts from ladies across the country."

"Oh," Becky said as she set the bucket down. The topic seemed to have piqued her interest. "Any luck?"

Carrie shook her head. "Not yet. But I have some options. I need to get it right this time and find someone that wants the same things as Peter. He's a really nice man."

"I know," Becky said. "I can't count the number of times that he has helped me."

Carrie smiled and lowered her head. She stared at the newspaper, wondering if she was being too rigid in her quest to find a bride for Peter. None of the letters had impressed her so far. The one thing Peter wanted was a big family, and none of the ladies she had seen had mentioned it in their advertisement. They talked about other interests, and some even went further to talk about their love for children, but none of them had said anything about wanting a big family, and Carrie needed to be sure before she wrote back. She knew the chances of finding another woman unable to bear children was remote, but she had this fear holding her back.

"You know what?" Becky asked, placing both hands on the wooden fence. "Something came to my mind immediately after you said that. I need to show you some letters."

Carrie walked over to Becky's side of the fence. "Letters?"

Becky nodded. "You see, I receive correspondence from my nephew, Percival, who is presently teaching in a small town in Virginia. While his letters are mostly filled with his affection for his fiancée, Doris, Percival once mentioned that a fellow teacher in the next town had expressed her desire to marry. Her name is Amy Randall. I recall this because Amy was a big help to Percival when he started teaching. I'm certain Percival mentioned that Amy is desperate to start her own big family and that she loved children so much."

"Really?" Carrie asked curiously. "And this Amy lady... she's nice?"

"Ah, that's what Percival says," Becky answered. "And given how big a help she has been to my dear nephew and his fiancé, I reckon he's telling the truth. Perhaps, you'd write to Amy first and see. That's the only way you can get to know her better, and see if she is a good match for Peter. Thinking about it, I think the schoolmarm and the miner will make a good match since they are both desperate to have big families."

"I don't know why, but I'm liking the idea already," Carrie said, delighted. "Say, Becky, can you please write to Percival on my behalf and tell him of our plan? I'm hoping he can act as an introduction between Amy and me. I am very interested in getting to know her. Being a teacher makes her a good match for Peter. Teachers are usually kind, and affectionate, especially towards children, are they not?"

"I reckon they are. I can tell you that Amy is exactly that," Becky said. "I will write to Percival right away and inform him that you will be writing to him too with regards to Amy. Once Percival informs Amy, then you and Amy can get to know each other. If Percival's description of her is true, then I'm almost certain you will like her too."

"Oh, thank you, Becky," Carrie said. "You have put my mind at ease. I'm hoping this turns out well."

"Me too," Becky answered.

Carrie watched Becky return to the house, thankful that she had opened up to her. She took one last look at the newspaper before folding it in half and shoving it back underneath her arm. There was no use for it for the time being. In fact, if everything went well with Amy, Carrie would have no use for the newspaper again.

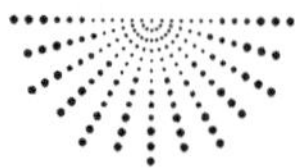

CHAPTER THREE

"*P*ercival, how could you?"

Amy Randal rose to her feet and brought both hands to her hips. Her eyebrows furrowed, and strands of her dull, brown hair tickled her forehead. She pushed her eyeglasses forward with her index finger and proceeded to glare at Percival, unable to believe her ears.

"Calm down, Amy, and think about it," Percival said, sitting in front of Amy's desk. "I'm sorry, but if you just take one moment to think about it, you'll realize that it's not such a terrible thing. In fact, it's not a bad thing at all."

"You haven't answered my question, how could you?" Amy repeated, her heart was pounding and a sick feeling had settled in her stomach. "How could you share something so personal about me... with your aunt? What was the topic of discussion for my marital status to come up?" Amy knew that her cheeks were red and she was clenching her fists. This was not fair!

"Amy..."

"Tell me, Percival," Amy almost shouted as her emotions threatened to overwhelm her.

It didn't sit right with Amy that Percival spoke about her desire to find a husband with his aunt. Someone she didn't even know. It was unsettling, perturbing. She knew Percival frequently wrote to his aunt, but the fact that he could easily give out such personal information about her, made her wonder what else he had written to his aunt about her.

"I'm telling Doris," Amy said, knowing that the words were childish but they just escaped her.

"Amy, you know I meant no harm." Percival looked so sorry. "You know my intentions were genuine, don't you?"

"That's my point, Percival. I don't know anything because you did it behind my back," Amy replied.

"You speak as if I stabbed you in the back, or gossiped for no reason," Percival said. "I was only trying to help."

"By telling your aunt everything about me?

"Yes," Percival answered. "It might not sound like it, but that's truly what it was. Now, will you sit down and let me explain what was running through my mind when I first sent her that letter?"

Reluctant at first, Amy clenched her jaw to prevent any more hash words and obliged. She proceeded to cross her arms and stare out the small window. "I'm listening."

"Thank you," Percival said and took a breath. "First things first, I sent my aunt that letter months ago, Amy. Back then, you had been so sad about being alone. You used to watch the parents come for their children at school and you'd just stare at them with a deep longing in your eyes and a frail, sad smile on your face. I could see you wanted that for yourself too. So, when you admitted to the fact that you were interested in having more of a family, I wrote to my aunt, mentioning it. I didn't think any harm would come of it, and I was right. I had a feeling my aunt would figure out a way to help."

"I don't need help," Amy said, knowing deep down that it was a lie.

"You don't need to pretend with me, Amy," Percival said. "I know you. Trust me when I say I was only trying to help. You are my close friend and all I want is for you to be happy."

Amy turned to him and leaned on the table. "Percival..."

"I know what you're going to say," Percival cut her off. "Being around these kids makes you happy, and you are content. But the truth is, I don't want you to be content, Amy. I want you to thrive. I want you to have what you want most in the entire world. Take Doris and I, for instance, did you ever think we were going to be this close to getting married?"

Amy chuckled and shook her head. "No."

"Me neither. At one point, I almost lost hope, but see how everything turned out," Percival told her. "Now, I cannot imagine my life without Doris and I am so happy."

"I haven't seen you this happy before."

"See?" Percival asked leaning forward. "Don't you want this kind of happiness too? Isn't the thought of love causing your heart to race? Are you not curious as to how you love, and what it feels like to be loved? Amy, this is what you want. Why aren't you more excited about this possibility?"

"Because even though I know you, I don't know your aunt or this... Carrie," Amy answered. "I don't know, Percival, this is a big risk."

"Well, obviously you don't," he said. "But that's fixable. You can get to know them. This is a great opportunity for you. Just stop and think about it. You know deep down, this is what you want."

"But it isn't," Amy said. "I admit that I really want to have a family, Percival. I mean, who doesn't dream of a family of their own? But not like this. I'm still pretty shocked that you spoke about me to your aunt. Now, you want me to travel all the way to Colorado, where I know no one?"

"Not immediately," he continued. "What I want from you right now is to communicate with Carrie. My aunt says that Carrie has engineered two successful marriages. Her son, and her son's friend. She found brides for them both and they are both very in love and very happy.

Somehow, Percival's statement piqued Amy's interest. "What do you mean she engineered two marriages?"

"Aunt Becky said Carrie wrote to her son's current wife and convinced her to move to Colorado. Then, apparently, her son's friend told her about his interest to start a family. Carrie arranged for another young lady to come all the way to Colorado and it turns out, that they were a perfect match too. Don't you think Carrie knows what she's doing?"

"Well…"

Amy scratched the back of her neck, unsure of what to say. Percival had made a valid point that had piqued her interest, was this possible? Two successfully arranged marriages? That couldn't have been easy to achieve. But if what Percival said was right, and Carrie did find brides for two gentlemen, then perhaps it was worth a chance. She would think this through before deciding if, or when, to get in touch with Carrie.

"Amy…" Percival said softly. "You've been my friend since I arrived here in Virginia from Colorado years ago. You helped me learn the ropes, helped me settle in and you've been a good friend. You've been a good friend to Doris too, and if you didn't introduce us to each other, we would never have met. Let me do this for you. I trust my aunt with my life. She's like a mother to me. I told her all the good things you've done for me too. If she thinks you can have a good life in Colorado, then why not take the chance? Or are you scared?"

"Of course not," Amy scoffed. "It's not fear, Percival." Which was silly; of course, she was afraid. Traveling across the country with nothing and no one she knew, was a big risk!

"I'm not asking you to go right away," he continued. "I'll mail your address and your first letter to Carrie, and from then on, you both can correspond and get to know each other. If after exchanging letters for a while, you still don't think you want to take the chance, then that's completely fine. Just promise me you'll at least try."

Amy rolled her eyes and smirked. Put like that it didn't sound too bad but she was going to make him pay just a little longer.

"Amy... promise me."

"Fine." Amy sighed. "I guess it won't hurt to try. I mean, if this goes well, then good for me. And if it doesn't, then I guess it wasn't meant to be."

Percival's announcement had woken something up in Amy. Something that felt like hope. It had been a while since she opened up her heart to anything. She had spent all her life in Virginia, and it had been okay but she always felt there was more. Perhaps, it was time for an adventure. Time to take charge of her life. A true family was what she wanted, and if Carrie could provide this for her, then Amy was willing to try.

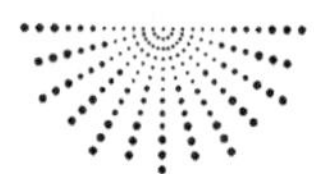

ear Carrie,

I hope this letter finds you well.

I cannot tell you how thrilled I am that you wrote back to me. Peter Quinn sounds like a wonderful man. I'm glad to hear that we have much in common. If I am being totally honest with you, I was skeptical about this endeavor. But over the past few weeks, I dare say I started to look forward to your letters.

I'm writing to you to tell you a bit about my background as we get to know each other. I am an orphan. I've been one since I was a little girl. My former schoolteacher, Miss McAnthony took me in when I was little, and cared for me. In fact, she was the reason I now have a passion for teaching.

I don't have any siblings. I was an only child, and I still am. So far in my life, I would say that when my parents passed away was one moment I would never forget. It was the first time I ever felt alone in the world. Growing up, the house was always quiet, and since I too was a quiet child, it was quite hard to get by.

I never want anyone in my family to experience this. It is the main reason I want to have a large family. I want my children to have someone else they can lean on, someone to talk to and share their burdens with. I want a home filled with children and their laughter.

Sharing this with you somehow made me feel lighter than I was before. Thank you for writing to me, Carrie. Truth be told, I haven't spoken about my past with anyone recently.

I look forward to hearing from you too. I would also like to know how Peter grew up. I'm available if you have questions. Please write back.

Yours truly,

Amy.

Carrie couldn't restrain herself from smiling. It was the same feeling. The very one she had when she had been exchanging letters about Drusilla with her old friend. Amy seemed like a nice girl. She ticked all her boxes, and she admitted that Peter seemed like the kind of man she wanted to be with. Carrie felt it in her bones that the two of them would be happy together. The letters between them had confirmed this and now that Amy was truly opening up to her she knew it was time.

The job was already done. The common ground had been established, all that was left was to send for Amy.

"Carrie?" Peter called her, walking into the living room. "Carrie, are you here?"

Carrie rose to her feet and turned to Peter with a smile on her face. "Yes, Peter. Come on in."

Hopeful and excited, Peter squinted his eyes and cautiously walked into the room. "You seem to be in a pretty good mood this morning, Carrie. I'm guessing the reason you called me here today has something to do with the request I made to you."

"It sure does," Carrie beamed. "Come in and sit, Peter. I have good news."

Peter chuckled and sat by Carrie's side. "I haven't even heard what you have to say, Carrie, but I'm excited already. Did you find me a bride?"

Carrie took in a deep breath and squeezed the letter in her hand before handing it to Peter. "I did, Peter. I'm pleased to say that I did."

Peter tilted his head to the side as she chuckled and he opened the letter. He took his time to read it, and the smile never faded from his face.

"Her name is Amy Randall, she is twenty-two years old, she lives in Virginia, and she's a teacher. I think she will be a good match for you," Carrie explained.

"And she's an orphan," Peter said, nodding. "Like I am."

"I will give you all the letters I received from Amy," Carrie continued. "That way you can get to know her better. We have been corresponding for weeks now. I like her, Peter. I think you'll like her too."

"Did she put out an advertisement in the paper?" Peter asked. "How did you get to know her?"

"From Becky," Carrie answered.

"Becky? Mrs. Montgomery, that lives next door?"

Carrie nodded. "Yes. Her nephew who lives in Virginia informed her that Amy was single, and looking to start a family. At first, I was skeptical. But after writing to her a few times, I am certain she's a good choice."

Peter sighed and carefully folded the letter, before putting it into his pocket. He interlocked his fingers and lowered his head, thinking.

"What's the matter, Peter?" Carrie asked, sensing his worry. "You don't look as thrilled as I thought you'd be. I would be lying if I claim you haven't been yourself the past few months. You are distant now, and I can tell that you're starting to get lonely. I think this will be good for you."

"It's what I want, there's no doubt about it," Peter said and sighed. "But what if it doesn't work out again? Carrie, I just realized something. I cannot go through what I went through with Gloria all over again. I mean, what if it doesn't work out again? I'm not saying I don't want to give it another shot, I'm saying..."

"You don't want to get hurt anymore."

"Yes," Peter said without hesitation. "I know it's something you, nor I can control. Yet, it doesn't stop how I feel. I'm scared of getting let down again, Carrie. I don't want to be optimistic, and then get disappointed. But still, I want a family. I sound like I have no idea what I want, I'm just so confused."

"I understand," Carrie said and took his hand. "However, I won't lie to you, nor will I sugarcoat things. We cannot control the future. I have no idea what will happen if you decide to send for Amy. I don't know if she will break your heart, but the only reason I want you to give Amy a chance is that I think she's going to be good for you if she is really who she says she is. She wants a big family like you. Becky vouchers for her too and tells me how nice she is. I get that same feeling. Give her a chance."

"She wants a big family too?" Peter asked softly.

Carrie nodded. "She does. Just like you. You have things in common already. You both like reading and sunsets. Give it a chance, Peter. I cannot guarantee you'd be happy in the long run, but it feels right to me. I want to be optimistic and believe that you will."

Peter exhaled. "All right then. If you believe Amy is the one for me, I have no reason to doubt you. I trust in your judgment, Carrie. Plus, I think I like Amy too after reading this letter."

Carrie patted his back. "Trust me, when you read the rest of the letters, you'll be certain."

"Then, it is settled. I will provide the necessary funds to send for Amy."

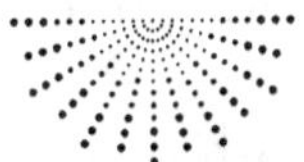

CHAPTER FIVE

"*D*idn't I tell you, Amy?" Percival said.

After placing her bags in the stagecoach, Amy took one last look at the school she had taught in for several years. She stood with her hands clasped together to keep them still, and smiled, knowing that she'd not only miss this place, but she would cherish the life she had here forever.

More than anything else, Amy was going to miss her students. They had a teary goodbye, and it took every last ounce of will in Amy's body not to cry. Her students had called her the best teacher they ever had, they had told Amy they loved her, and that they were going to miss her too. For a moment, Amy actually considered staying because of them. But a bigger part of her really wanted to go.

"All right now, don't start bragging about it," Amy said and rolled her eyes. "But, yes. You did tell me, Percival. I'm glad you did. I'm glad you told your aunt about me."

Percival stared at her with a proud look on his face. "I'm glad I did. I can't believe you're actually leaving Virginia for the first time. I'm going to miss you, my dear friend."

"Not as much as I will miss you, Percival," Amy responded. "You have been a great friend to me."

"Ah, I should be saying this to you, not the other way around," Percival answered. "If I start to count all the good things that you did for me, I'm afraid I won't recall them all. My time here in Virginia was only possible because of you, and all that you did. I won't forget this. Neither will I forget you, Amy."

Amy felt tears sting her eyes. She took off her glasses, rubbed away the tears, and then put them on again. "Thank you, Percival."

"You're welcome." He smiled. "Plus, I pray you don't come back. Not in a bad way... I mean, if you don't come back, then it would mean all went well. Write to me though. We must keep in touch."

"We must," Amy said, nodding. "I hope all goes well too. I didn't think this was something I was open to at first, but Carrie has truly reassured me. Everything she said about Peter makes me feel as if it is right, and seeing as Peter is paying to bring me to Colorado, it confirms that he's serious about this. It makes me excited that they heard my story, and they want me to be Peter's bride."

"You'll do well," Percival said and tapped her on the shoulder. "Doris sends her regards. She wanted to come herself and bid you a final farewell, but she's unable to leave the shop."

"Oh, Doris and I already said goodbye yesterday," Amy said. "She refused to leave my side. There's a deadline she has to meet today, so I understand. I'll make sure to write to the both of you as soon as I arrive in Gray Rock."

"Be careful, Amy. You know what you want, make sure you don't sacrifice that. If you get to Colorado, and things don't work out, come back. This is the only home you know. Now, I really hope Colorado becomes your new home, where you build your own family, but if things don't go according to your plan... come home."

"I will," Amy whispered. "I'll make things work." For a moment her courage failed her and doubt clouded her mind. "Even though I have some information about

Peter, I'm still nervous. There are many questions in my head, and you know how I can get when I'm tense. However, seeing that I'm able to put all of that aside, and go after this, I can only hope that it's to achieve a permanent state of happiness. Thank you, Percival. I'll be in touch. Hopefully, we'll have a good cause to see each other soon."

"Hopefully," Percival said. "Have a safe trip, Amy."

"Thank you. Take care of my kids while I'm gone."

"They'll be fine."

With that, Amy hopped into the stagecoach and waved at Percival as the horses surged and the coach rolled down the street. Once he was out of her sight, she sat back and smiled to herself. In as much as Virginia was the only place she knew, the thought of visiting Colorado caused a fluttery feeling of hope in her stomach.

Frankly, looking back at the past few weeks, Amy found it almost unbelievable that she had changed her mind so quickly. She recalled how skeptical she had been about Percival's suggestion from the start. But it only took one letter from Carrie to change Amy's mind. Now, all she could think of was what her future in Gray Rock,

Colorado was going to look like. She had daydreamed about it, created fake scenarios in her head, and caught herself imagining what Peter Quinn and their future children would look like.

Starting a family had been a vision of Amy's for as long as she could remember. Now that it was slowly materializing, she started to feel the tension. Amy had reached a turning point in her life. There were only two ways it could go. She could find happiness as she craved, or she could end up disappointed.

For now, she would try to enjoy the journey.

After spending half a day on the stagecoach and then days on a train, Amy ended her journey on another stagecoach. It finally came to a halt at her final destination. She had been so lost in her own thoughts, that it didn't feel like that much time had passed at all, though her body was stiff and dusty. However, the more time she spent on the road, the more intense her worrying became. Even though she tried to brush it off, it still lingered.

What if Peter didn't like her? She was plain, maybe a little too plain. What if he was awful or mean? What if she couldn't love him? What if no one turned up?

Amy sat in the coach as her case was unloaded. She knew what to do next, but just couldn't seem to move. Carrie had explained to her that when she arrived, she was to get off the stagecoach at the entrance of the town. There, Peter would be waiting for her. Amy could see people waiting, but she couldn't move. There was a lump in her throat, one that had gotten significantly bigger since she left Virginia.

"Ma'am, we're here," the driver called holding the door for her.

It took Amy a moment before she finally took a step forward and was helped down. She smiled and gave her thanks to the driver and took another step. After the first step, it was easier to move. She shook her head vigorously to ward off the intrusive thoughts and looked around. Amy tried to convince herself that there was nothing to worry about. Since Peter sent for her, he was interested. She wasn't going to meet a complete stranger.

Yet, that was exactly what she was doing. Amy took off her glasses and leaned on the door of the stagecoach. There were some questions she should have covered with Carrie that she didn't. What kind of woman was Peter hoping to receive? A ravishing beauty? A tall, slender woman with blonde hair and blue eyes?

Amy was none of these things. Or at least, she didn't consider herself to be. All her life, she had thought of her looks as ordinary. That was what it was. Her brown hair was dull, and her equally brown eyes didn't sparkle as much as she would have liked them to. She wore thick glasses which she had forgotten to mention. Amy was of average height, and pretty petite. However, her looks were very ordinary. She was not a woman who would amaze Peter.

Amy scanned the dress she had on and sighed. She had chosen a yellow floral gown, pretty; in fact, her best but a little faded. If she had thought about her appearance before she left Virginia, perhaps, she would have put some more thought into picking out a new dress and styling her hair. It was too late to change anything. Amy could only hope that Peter didn't hold high expectations. She didn't want to see a look of disappointment in his eyes during their first meeting. It would break her.

To further increase her worrying, Amy couldn't help but wonder if wanting many children was the only tangible thing she and Peter had in common. Was that where their similarities ended? Was it enough to create a life time bond? What if it wasn't enough? What if Peter simply accepted her as a wife because he wanted children, and the marriage in time ended up lonely and loveless? That would defeat the purpose of her move to Gray Rock. After all, ultimately, she wanted to find love.

"Oh dear," Amy whispered, feeling her stomach twist into knots.

CHAPTER SIX

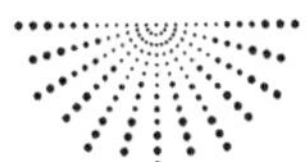

Amy swallowed hard and scanned her surroundings. Other passengers from the stagecoach were already walking away.

The town didn't look like much, but she figured they were still on the outskirts, so it wasn't right to judge so quickly. From the look of it, Gray Rock seemed like a peaceful town. Amy only hoped that she was right. She had traveled a long way.

A few people were on the streets, cowboys and a few horses. Amy watched the stagecoach disappear around a corner. She stood with her bag, pushed her eyeglasses further up her nose, and let out a nervous breath. There were other people there, waiting with their wagons. Amy scanned their faces, hoping to see if one of them matched Carrie's description of Peter.

"Freya?"

Amy heard someone say from behind her. She turned around and her eyes fell on a bald-headed man with blue eyes.

"I'm sorry?" Amy responded.

"Are you Freya? I'm Austin."

"Oh, no," Amy said and shook her head. "I'm afraid you have the wrong person."

"Oh, really?" the man asked.

"I'm certain. My name is Amy."

"My apologies," he said and walked back to his wagon.

Amy turned back around, and the first person her eyes fell on matched Carrie's description perfectly. The man had curly dark brown hair, brown eyes, a big build, and a neatly trimmed beard. A smile slowly formed on Amy's lips. Carrie had failed to mention that Peter was incredibly handsome and so tall.

Holding her breath, Amy walked up to him and tapped him on the shoulder. "Peter? Peter Quinn?"

The man turned to her slowly and tilted his head to the side, assessing her. He stretched his hand to her and smiled softly. "Amy Randall?"

"Yes," Amy said excitedly. Nervously, her hand flew to her face and adjusted her glasses. "I'm Amy. Goodness, it's really nice to meet you."

Noticing she was acting overly eager, Amy reined in her excitement and shook his hand. He was smiling at her, but his expression hadn't changed that much. There was no look of joy! Amy couldn't tell what he was thinking. Was all her worrying valid?

"It's a pleasure to meet you, Amy. Thank you so much for coming all this way," Peter said.

Did he not mind that she didn't look half as pretty as he did? Amy swallowed and placed both hands behind her. She had received compliments in the past about her charming smile, and nice skin. Many had told her that she was pretty though she didn't believe them. Even though Amy figured she looked like every ordinary girl, she hoped that Peter would be impressed. She had only met Peter for a few seconds and she was already very attracted to him. It would be unfair to Peter if he wasn't pleased with her.

But he wasn't saying anything. Peter walked past her and began to load her bag into the wagon.

"You look really nice," Amy told him. "Carrie described you well."

"Thank you," he said, chuckling. "Are you all right? How was the journey? I hope it wasn't so stressful."

"Oh, it was long," Amy answered. "But time went by quickly."

"Are you hungry?" Peter asked. "We could stop by a diner to eat before I take you to Carrie's home."

"Oh, I'm not hungry," Amy answered, feeling awkward and unsure of what to say. "But thank you. I brought something to eat in the coach from the last stop."

Peter nodded. "Thank you again, Amy, for coming all this way. I will do my best to make sure you're comfortable and I look forward to getting to know you better."

Amy placed both hands on her cheeks before they flushed crimson. "I look forward to it too. Thank you, Peter. I feel welcome already."

"I'm glad," he answered and smiled. *My, it was a beautiful smile!*

When he was done loading his wagon with her bag, Peter helped Amy into the seat and set the horses into motion. The silence between them was not awkward, but it still made Amy uneasy.

"So," Amy said and glanced at him. "Did you wait long?"

Peter shook his head. "I didn't."

"Yes, you did."

Her response caused him to stare at her. "I really didn't wait long."

"If you say so," Amy said, giggling with nerves. She had no idea why she thought to tease Peter, but it felt nice talking to him like they were already acquainted.

"Fine, you're right," Peter admitted. "I had been waiting there for about an hour before your stagecoach arrived. But I didn't think it mattered."

Amy smiled to herself. "I was just curious, that's all. I'm sorry you had to wait for so long."

"It's no problem," Peter answered. "I liked waiting. It built the anticipation for your arrival. Besides, I'd much prefer waiting for you, then keeping you waiting."

"That's a nice thing to say. It would have been worrying to find no one there."

"It is?" Peter chuckled. "Ah, well. By the way, how'd you know I wasn't being truthful?"

Amy shrugged her shoulders. "I didn't know. I was just guessing. But it actually seemed as though you had been standing there for some time. If you had just arrived, then you'd have been alert, and trying to spot me. But when I arrived you were lost in thought. It was easy to guess that you'd been there for a while."

"Oh," was all Peter said as he tilted his head to the side. "You're very observant. I'm guessing that's why you're a good teacher. Carrie said you taught little kids back in Virginia."

"I did," Amy answered. "I'll tell you all about it. That is... if you want."

Peter met her gaze. "I'd like to hear all about it, Amy. I love children."

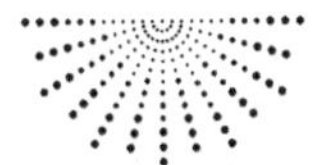

CHAPTER SEVEN

Amy was not how Peter had imagined she'd be.

In fact, Peter had not even visualized her in his head at all. Strangely, he had not imagined what she looked like. All he was after was meeting her and taking her to Carrie's.

Seeing her for the first time made him realize that the image of Gloria arriving in Gray Rock with Steven was the only thing on his mind as regards Amy's looks. It was silly and the reality was different. Amy wasn't Gloria. She didn't look like her one bit, and it was embarrassing that he had concluded that she would.

Still, that didn't change a thing. Peter was caught off guard at first, but when Amy smiled, and he saw the patient excitement in her eyes, it felt as if the gates of his heart had opened to her. He was supposed to give her the warm welcome, yet it felt like he got the warmth from her instead. Like she was the one greeting him. It felt nice having hope again. Their first meeting had gone better than Peter had expected. Amy was smart, she was pretty, cute, and charming. The sound of her voice was beautiful and he liked how she spoke. He could listen to her all day.

They arrived at Carrie's home shortly after Peter picked Amy up. Carrie had suggested that Amy stay in a spare room in her home first. It would not be suitable for her to stay with Peter, but he understood and didn't object. Given the events that had influenced their lives months back, Peter needed to provide Amy with a safe place to stay. Though he could have slept outside, he wasn't at home all the time, hence letting Amy live with Carrie until they exchanged their vows seemed like a better option. It was best if they started slow, and got to know each other. Even though Amy seemed like the kind of woman he wanted to be with, Peter still wanted to tread carefully. He feared that if he got disappointed and heartbroken again, it would be the end of his dreams. This might just be his final attempt to find a bride. No matter how it ended.

"Amy!" Carrie beamed immediately as she opened the front door. "Oh, my goodness. Hello!"

Amy smiled and was engulfed by Carrie in a brief hug. "You must be Mrs. Carrie McCord. It's a pleasure to meet you."

"Please, just call me Carrie," she answered. "Come in, come in! I hope your journey went well?"

"It sure did," Amy said. "I've never traveled this far before. It was very exciting."

"I'm glad to hear," she replied. "Peter, be a darling and take Amy's bag to the spare room beside mine."

"Of course," Peter said, giving Amy one last look before making his way across the living room with the bag in his hands.

On his way down the hall, Drusilla appeared from her room, stopping Peter in his tracks. Peter smiled at her and dropped the bag to the floor.

"Drusilla, how are you today? How's the baby doing? Has he kicked again?"

"I'm fine, Peter," she answered, looking over his shoulder. "No, the baby has been pretty quiet these last few days. That aside, I heard voices."

Peter raised his eyebrows. "You left your bed because you heard voices?"

Drusilla nodded affirmatively. "Has Amy arrived? Is she in the living room with Carrie?"

"Yes," Peter said.

Drusilla clapped excitedly. "Come on, move. I must welcome her."

Peter sighed and moved to the side, a feeling of worry growing in his gut. "Seeing how you and Carrie are reacting to Amy's presence makes me feel terrible. I mean, I was glad to meet her too, but what if she thinks I wasn't as excited as you and Carrie when I should be the most excited one since she's going to be my bride?"

Drusilla paused and placed a hand on her rotund stomach. "What do you mean? Did you not welcome her properly?"

"I did," Peter said. "Well... I thought I did. But now that I really think about it, was I too casual? Should I have probably given her a hug instead of a handshake?"

Drusilla patted Peter on the shoulder. "You worry too much, my friend. I'm sure Amy didn't overthink it. Plus, you have plenty of time to convince her that you mean well. She came here for you. Don't worry too much too soon, that will just make you nervous."

Peter thought about it, then nodded. "You're right. I'm probably overthinking it. Thank you, Drusilla."

Drusilla took a step closer to Peter. "So, what's your first impression of Amy?"

"She's nice," he said, unable to stop his grin. "We had a brief chat on our way here, and I really liked our conversation. She's pretty too."

"Good," Drusilla beamed at him and stepped back. "You're off to a great start. Now, I must introduce myself to Amy. We have a new addition to the house, so it's going to be a party of four, every day."

Peter squinted his eyes. "A party of four?"

"Yes. Carrie, Gloria, Amy, and I," Drusilla answered. "Drop her bag and join us out there."

With that said, Drusilla made her way to the living room while Peter took the bag to the spare room. Once he had set it down in the corner, he walked back out into the living room to find Amy and Drusilla in a cheery conversation.

"Drusilla... I really like your name," Amy said, beaming. Her gaze remained lowered for some reason. She didn't stare into Drusilla's eyes for more than two seconds.

"Thank you," Drusilla voiced. "You have a nice name too."

"Oh, please. Amy is a very ordinary, and common name. Unlike yours," Amy said and lowered her gaze again.

Peter moved closer to them. Close enough to assess Amy and figure out why she was looking away, but still keeping his distance, so his presence didn't affect their conversation.

"Are you hungry?" Drusilla asked her. "We made some soup for you."

Amy raised her eyes. "At the moment, I'm all right. But thank you so much for the effort. I'll have the soup for dinner."

It was after the third time Amy did it, that Peter finally realized why her gaze was darting. Amy was staring at Drusilla's stomach. In fact, she wasn't just staring... she was admiring Drusilla's rounded stomach. Almost as if she wanted to touch it.

Almost as if Drusilla read Amy's mind, she placed her hand on her stomach. "I'm seven months or thereabouts," she announced, caressing her stomach. "Anytime now, this baby... who has been the cause of many sleepless nights... will arrive in this world. I'm so excited. Jamison and I are counting the days until our blessed baby is in our arms."

"I can only imagine," Amy said, smiling. "You must be so excited."

Drusilla nodded. "That and many other emotions. It's a blessing, but I have to admit I'm scared too. Will I be a good mother?"

Peter looked in Amy's direction at the same time she lifted her gaze to steal a glance at him. His heart skipped a beat when their eyes met and he immediately looked away. Recalling that Amy couldn't wait to have her own children too caused him to smile. That was only one of the differences between Gloria and Amy. The latter shared his desire to have a home filled with children. Just like him. He also found her easier to talk to and just as pretty. This was turning out so amazing that he felt his heart filled with gratitude.

Amy pushed her glasses up from the bridge of her nose and blushed. "I know we just met, but I'm happy for you."

"Thank you, Amy," Drusilla answered. "That means a lot. I have a good feeling we will get along well and become firm friends."

There was something about the way Amy adjusted her glasses that gave Peter the tingles. She was already pretty, but when she used her index finger to push up her glasses, Peter couldn't help but smile. Perhaps, he had been worried for nothing after all. All he had to do was put his doubts aside and accept that Amy was going to be the woman he desired.

"All right now," Carrie said, walking into the living room. "Drusilla, do you want to show Amy to her room, or do you want me to do it?"

"I'll do it, Carrie," Drusilla answered. "I'd love to. Let's go, Amy. You can freshen up and prepare for dinner. Jamison will be back from the mines shortly."

CHAPTER EIGHT

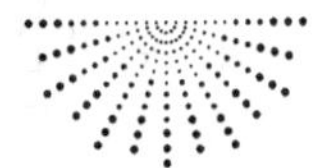

Amy sat on the soft bed and ran her fingers over the smooth sheet. The room had a small window that allowed for the bright rays of the sun to fill it. The square-shaped room wasn't as big as Amy's bedroom back in Virginia, but it was a decent size and nice with a dresser and a wardrobe. This was a place she could get used to.

The reception she had received had been even better than she had thought it was going to be. Amy was taken aback at first when Carrie and Drusilla welcomed her in such a pleasant, and joyful manner. One would think that they had already met before. It made Amy even happier when she saw that Drusilla was pregnant.

Somehow, everything about the home pleased her, especially Peter. It was a good start.

"If you need anything at all, please don't hesitate to ask," Drusilla told her and sat by her side.

"Thank you," Amy answered. "But can I ask you questions instead?"

"Of course," she answered, nodding. "You can ask me anything."

Amy adjusted where she sat and faced Drusilla. "Do you know Peter well?"

Drusilla paused. "Well, you could say that. I moved here almost a year ago, and we have been good friends ever since. So, yes, I reckon I know Peter well."

"Carrie has told me what he is like, but if I were to ask you the same thing, what would you say about Peter? How long has he wanted to marry?"

"Well, let's see..." Drusilla mumbled. "Peter is an amazing man, Amy. He is a really good friend to us, so I can imagine he will be wonderful to you, his bride. When I first got here, Peter was one of the first people that welcomed me. I'll never forget it. You have nothing to worry about. He's wanted to marry, at least out loud, since I married Jamison. Having read your letters he never hesitated in asking that you come all the way, because of this, I'm almost certain that all will go well."

Amy sighed and nodded. "I hope so. This is my first time leaving Virginia. When Percival, my good friend, told me about Carrie, I was very skeptical. At first, a little angry that he would discuss me behind my back! I didn't want to take a risk. In fact, it's strange that I came all this way. I'm not one who usually takes risks."

"I can say the same thing," Drusilla said. "I moved all the way from Connecticut to Colorado because of Carrie. I used to be a maid, you see, and there was a point in my life when I had to make a decision. My friend told me about Carrie and Gray Rock, and I was so skeptical." Drusilla let out a sigh and then smiled a contented smile and her hand went to her stomach. "I didn't want to take the risk. But here I am. I couldn't have made a better decision. My life is great here. I am married... happily, I have a child on the way and good friends like Peter. What more could I ask for?"

"I think Peter is a good man too," Amy said. "I mean, we've only met briefly, but he seems to have my best interest at heart. That's enough for me. Even though I want to get married, I don't just want to do it recklessly. I want a marriage filled with love. I think it's important for a happy family that the couple love each other. I mean, how could one possibly teach their children about love if they haven't experienced it themselves?"

"I completely agree with you," Drusilla answered. "Love is paramount. I'm certain that once you and Peter get to know each other better, falling in love will be easy. I see a connection between the two of you already."

"You think so?" Amy asked, blushing.

Drusilla nodded, affirmatively. "I do. I'm sure Carrie was certain you'd be a good match for Peter before sending for you. You can trust Carrie's judgment. Since you're here, it means you and Peter have a lot in common."

"But what if that's not enough?" Amy asked. "What if having a good connection with Peter, and having things in common isn't enough? I mean, it's possible that we both like each other, and are comfortable around each other, yet we're not in love?" Amy was afraid of this the most and she bit her lip to stop the tears that threatened to spill down her face.

Drusilla took her time to respond. She looked away, almost as if she was thinking of something. "That is true too," she finally said. "It's possible to have a connection with someone and not feel love. Peter knows this. But, you won't know how things will turn out until you try. All this thinking won't get you anywhere. Take it from me. Just live in the present. Let things play out how they should."

"I'm sorry," Amy said, shaking her head. "I got so serious with you."

"No, don't apologize," Drusilla told her. "I understand your worries. Believe me. You just moved across the country, to a new town where you know no one. It's only normal that you have questions. I might not be great at answering them, but I assure you, your worries are very valid. I had them myself! However, over time, you will see that you have nothing to worry about."

Amy met Drusilla's gaze and nodded. "I hope so."

"Good," Drusilla told her. "Now, I showed you the house earlier. Change out of these dusty clothes, I will fetch you some water from the pump and you can freshen up, and rest... make sure you sleep, and then when you think you're fully refreshed, you can join us."

"Thank you, Drusilla," Amy said. "Truly. You have all been so nice to me."

"You're welcome, Amy. I'll leave you for now."

When Drusilla left the room, Amy lay on the bed. Drusilla was right about the fact that worrying would get her nowhere. She had come all the way to Gray Rock. The least Amy could do was ignore the lingering doubts, and be hopeful about the prospects of her future.

CHAPTER NINE

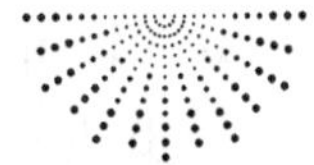

"**I** hope you have better information for me this time, Austin."

In the next town, an hour away from Gray Rock, Mitch Stock was seated on a wooden table in a run-down boarding house. The men, who were now under his command, were standing around the room, all paying attention to the conversation. Seven months had passed since Albie had gone to prison. All their efforts to get him out had been to no avail.

It took them seven months to plan their revenge. Seven months to gather money, and weapons. If only Albie had listened to Mitch when he asked that they took their time to prepare, he would have been with them at that very moment, when all was set to enact their vengeance.

"I do, Mitch," Austin said and sat down on the bed.

"I'll decide if it's good information," Mitch retorted. "Now, let's hear it. What goes on in Gray Rock?"

"The couples live happily in the town," Austin started. "Jamison McCord, Eugene Tompkins, and their wives still live in Gray Rock, and they have no intention of leaving anytime soon."

"You're off to a bad start, Austin. This is basic information. Not something that would benefit me in any way," Mitch lashed his tongue at him. "Tell me something I don't know."

Austin scanned the room. "All right. You know Peter? Peter Quinn. The third man? Well, apparently, he has found a bride. A woman arrived in town yesterday and he welcomed her himself."

Mitch interlocked his fingers. "Peter Quinn? Wasn't he the one that got married seven months ago?"

"No. That was Eugene Tompkins. Apparently, Eugene stole Peter's bride."

"Are you sure of this?"

"Yes. I was at the entrance of the town when the replacement woman arrived. Her name is Amy. If all goes well, they are set to be married soon."

"A wedding is a great place to catch them by surprise, boss," Dean, one of the gang members voiced. "They won't see us coming."

"And they will all be in one place, with no weapons," Chase, another gang member added. "What better place to catch them by surprise."

Dean nodded and glanced at Chase. "It's the opportunity we have been waiting for. We always failed because once we attack one of them, the others see us coming. Like the last time, when we caught that lady in the woods, and the miners surrounded us. Or how Albie got arrested. They are always prepared and they come after us. But this time, we go after them. They will all be at the wedding. All the miners, the wives, Jamison, Eugene, Peter... we can take back our town once and for all."

"What if you get arrested like Albie?" Austin asked. "The new sheriff is strict. That's how they were able to send Albie to jail. I heard he has it out for the rest of the gang. People in the town say he's been searching for you all."

Mitch scoffed. "He won't find us. He might be strict and smart, but he can't apprehend us if he doesn't see us coming," he said. "We will be in and out of the place as fast as we can. I'll divide you into groups of two, and give you a specific target. You are to only shoot at them during the wedding. I don't care if there are casualties. Make sure you get revenge on the people that ruined our gang. We must not fail. We only have one shot at this."

"What's our plan after we get our revenge?" Chase asked. "I mean, if we think about it, after we have our revenge, the sheriff will be on our tail. We will have to go back into hiding."

"That will only be for a while," Mitch told him and rose to his feet. "If the sheriff hunts us for too long, we will get rid of him too. Nothing can stand in our way. We used to control that town. Everyone cowered in fear when we were in charge. We must get that respect back. For Albie's sake."

They all nodded in approval and mumbled amongst themselves.

"How many guns are at our disposal, Dean?"

"Five guns, boss," he answered.

"It's enough. I would have preferred that each one of you had a gun, but we must not put this off any longer. We will pick the best men amongst us with a good aim, and you will be given your targets. You will be paired with someone else too. That person will be watching your back until your task is complete."

"But Mitch," Chase spoke up. "We are a total of nine men left. You included. Austin won't join us, so we are short of one man for your plan to work."

"I will work alone," Mitch said. "I don't need anyone watching my back. Austin, I need you to find out exactly where and when this wedding is going to be held. Since you are close to the miners, it shouldn't be that hard to get this information."

Austin rose from the bed. "I'll make inquiries and I'll let you know as soon as I have confirmation on the details."

"Good. Chase, give him his due and you can be on your way," Mitch said.

The wedding couldn't come at a better time. They had discussed various plans for months and decided that the best way to get revenge on them was to get them all together, in one place. The miners, and their wives. After several months, the perfect opportunity just fell right into their laps. The fools would not see them coming.

"Listen up, all of you," Mitch said after Austin took his leave. "This is a once-in-a-blue-moon opportunity. Whatever we do, we must get it right. Getting our revenge is the first step in taking our town back and making Albie proud. Anyone that tries to stand in our way will be gunned down. As I said, we must not fail."

Murmurs of agreement went through the men.

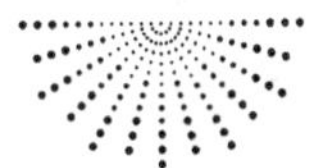

Amy sat between Peter and Carrie at the dining table, listening to them chat about their day. It was her first dinner with all of them. Her second meeting with Peter. The day before, when she arrived, Amy was meant to join them for dinner, but she had fallen asleep even before she had the chance to freshen up. Amy hadn't realized she was so tired from her travel, until she woke up the next morning, confused. It took her a couple of minutes to realize where she was. After profoundly apologizing to Carrie and Drusilla for not joining them for dinner, Amy prepared for the day and even joined Carrie in the kitchen at some point.

The day had gone by very quickly. One minute they were talking about Amy's journey, and the next minute, it was dinner time. Drusilla had barely come out of her room the whole day. Amy had hoped to pay her a visit and ask how the mother and unborn child were faring, but she didn't get the chance to before Drusilla joined them at the table to eat.

"Amy, are you all right?" Peter whispered to her with a concerned look on his face. "I'm sorry if this is a bit... too much. Carrie always hosts a dinner for all of us friends once every week, and it just happened to..."

"Peter," Amy said, instinctively reaching for, and squeezing his arm. "It's all right. I don't mind at all."

"Are you sure? This is just us, but you should see it when she hosts all the miners."

"I don't mind." Amy smiled. "Everyone is really nice to me and I like listening to the stories. This all seems exciting to me, but good at the same time. It's thrilling."

"Good... then. As long as you're fine," Peter said. "If you need anything, ask me, I'm here for you."

Amy nodded in response and diverted her attention to her plate of food. Carrie had made them some delicious mashed potatoes, beef, beans, and some gravy. Amy had helped in the little way that she could by helping while Carrie cooked. It took a lot of convincing from her before

Carrie let her work, but in the end, they both enjoyed their time together, cooking and talking in the kitchen.

"So, Amy," Eugene said, grabbing her attention. "Would you mind telling us a bit about yourself? You don't have to if you don't want to. It just feels as though you haven't said anything. What was growing up in Virginia like for you?"

Amy scanned their faces, noticing that they were all staring at her keenly. She cleared her throat and straightened her back, biting down her nerves as she tried to think.

"Well, where do I start?" Amy mumbled. "I don't have a... wholesome story to tell you about my childhood. Growing up was difficult for me. When people say they want to go back to being a child so they can relive what it felt like to be free from responsibilities again, I find it hard to relate to them."

The room had gone silent now. They all just stared at her with rapt attention. Amy stole glances at them, scared that she had ruined the mood. But since they asked, she had to keep going.

"What I mean is," Amy continued. "Life wasn't a bed of roses for me because I was orphaned at a young age. A very young age. I don't remember the time before it or my parents and I had no relatives, so most times I had to beg to eat. My eyesight isn't that great, so I would always bump into things, or drop things when I tried to work and people called me clumsy and refused to let me do anything for them to earn some money. There were times I would go days without eating. Goodness, I'm not even sure how I survived..."

A lump formed in Amy's throat and tears stung her eyes. It was a reflex reaction, one that only happened when she thought about the past and how cold and hungry she had been all the time.

"All of that changed when Mary McAnthony, a school-teacher, took me in and cared for me. That was when life finally felt... worth living. She fed and clothed me, taught me to read and write, and over time, she taught me the ropes of teaching. When she retired, I took over her job and the rest they say is history. I survived, and I'm still surviving."

It was obvious that she had darkened the mood in the room. Amy took off her glasses and wiped the tears from the corner of her eyes. She didn't want to meet any of their gazes. Amy was afraid she might cry if she saw how sorry they looked for her.

"I'm so sorry, Amy," Gloria said, breaking the silence. "You're a strong woman. Not everyone would have been able to endure what you did. It must have been really lonely during that period."

"I'm glad you're here now," Drusilla said. "I'm thankful, actually."

Amy drew in a shuddery breath. "Thank you, but I did not mean to ruin the mood."

"It's all right," Peter cut her off and took her hand. "How about we go for a stroll before dessert? To take your mind off of things?"

Amy lifted her head. "I'd like that," she said, almost in a whisper.

Holding her hand, Peter rose to his feet and pushed the chair aside for her to move. He asked that they be excused before ushering Amy out of the house.

As soon as Amy stepped out of the house and felt the wind on her face, she immediately felt refreshed. The corner of her lips tilted up when she looked down and noticed that Peter had not let go of her hand. They walked into the yard in silence, taking small steps.

"I didn't mean to ruin the mood," Amy finally said as they approached the fence. "I really didn't imagine the room would go silent when I talked about my childhood."

Peter chuckled softly. "It's not your fault. It is sad, though. As Gloria said, it must have been lonely."

"Oh, it was," Amy answered. "Right now, I only have two friends in Virginia. Percival, the reason I was able to hear about you in the first place, and his fiancé, Doris... and my children of course. They were wonderful but life was still difficult up until I left Virginia. What I always did was take every day as it came. That was how I was able to live."

"I commend you. Really. Enduring the hardships that you were forced to go through had to have been exhausting. But the fact that you found your way, you can teach children, and stand on your own two feet says a lot about your character. It says a lot about the woman I intend to marry. About how strong and brave she is."

Amy bit her lower lip and lowered her head. "Thank you. That means so much, coming from you."

"You mentioned that you only have two friends in Virginia. You never tried courting anyone?" Peter asked.

"No." Amy shook her head "Well, this is my first... courtship. I'm hoping it will be my last."

Peter squeezed her hand, causing tingles to run up her spine, and then held out his arm for her to take. "I hope so too," he said with a charming smile on his face.

They came to a halt at the fence. "What about you? Have you ever been in love before?"

Peter inhaled sharply and leaned on the fence. "No. I've never been in love. Even though I really want children as soon as possible, I cannot bring myself to get married without falling in love first. Liking someone is not enough."

Amy felt warm inside, hearing Peter speak her mind. "I feel the same way too."

"Seeing as I am already imagining a future with you that's keeping me up all night, smiling to myself, I really think I'm on the right path. I'm glad you came here, Amy."

Amy wanted to tell him that she was glad he chose her, but she couldn't speak. When Percival told her months ago that he fell in love with Doris at first sight, she didn't believe him. How could you possibly love someone you just met?

However, standing there, staring into Peter's eyes made everything so clear. It was possible. She had done it.

"May I" Peter swallowed and scratched his neck.

"May you what?" Amy asked, taking a step closer.

"May I kiss you, Amy?" he asked.

Without hesitation, Amy held her breath and nodded in response. She stood still, as Peter took off his hat and leaned in. Just when she felt his breath on her skin when his lips were only inches from hers, the sound of shouting men had them jumping away from each other. Amy gasped, she was scared to bits.

Instinctively, Peter put his hand out and directed Amy behind him. He stood in front of her, scanning the yard to figure out the cause of the commotion.

Amy could barely breathe. She didn't know which action actually stole her breath. The sound of panic or the fluttering feeling in her heart seeing how protective Peter was over her.

"It's some men from the saloon," Peter announced and sighed in relief. He still had his back to her, making sure that there was no cause for concern. "They are probably just blowing off steam. It's nothing to worry about."

Touched by how quick Peter was to jump in to protect her, Amy wrapped her hands around his waist and hugged him tightly from behind. Peter didn't move or protest. He simply placed his hand over hers and remained still. They stayed that way for a while, as Amy basked in the warmth of Peter's body.

CHAPTER ELEVEN

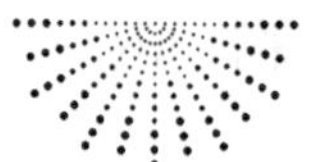

ONE WEEK LATER...

"**W**ell, you mentioned you liked lilies because yellow is your favorite color, so I bought them for you."

Amy sniffed the flowers and smiled. "Thank you, Peter. They are beautiful."

"I'm glad you like them," he answered, smiling sheepishly. "Have you had something to eat this afternoon?"

Amy nodded, still sniffing the flowers. "I have."

"That's good. If you don't have plans for dinner, I would like to take you to this diner near the mercantile. It's my favorite one. I'm sure you'll like it too. Or you might not... I just think that since their food is... well, I figured since you like..."

"Peter, I'm sure I'll love it," Amy said, unable to control her giggling at his nerves. "I'll see you soon?"

"Yes," Peter said after taking in a deep breath. "I will be back in a few hours. I have to return to the mine and finish up my work for the day. If you need anything, send for me, anytime."

"I'll be fine," Amy said to him. "Be safe."

"You too."

Amy waited for Peter to disappear into the street before she walked back inside to join Drusilla and Gloria. They had spent the past three days looking for a dress Amy could get married in and Drusilla had called them all to her room, stating that she had found the best dress.

"Amy, what took you so long?" Drusilla asked, hiding the dress behind her.

"I'm sorry. Peter brought me flowers," Amy beamed, setting the flowers down on the bed. "I can't wait to see the dress."

"Hello, Amy."

Amy turned to Gloria and greeted her first with a smile. "Hi, Gloria. How are you?"

"Oh, that's right," Drusilla said. "You both haven't officially met."

"We have been introduced to each other during dinner the other day," Amy voiced. "We just haven't had a one-on-one discussion before."

"Steven has been unwell for the past week, so Gloria has been spending more time than usual looking after him," Drusilla said. "She could only come over today because Steven was feeling so much better and wanted to go with his father to the mine."

"Oh," Amy said, sitting by Gloria's side. "I am so sorry to hear this. Is he still running a fever?"

"Oh, give me one moment," Drusilla said, making her way to the door. "I'll be back. I really need to pee. I'm afraid this child is using my bladder as a pillow."

Amy and Gloria both chuckled in response. Gloria sighed and diverted her attention to Amy.

"His fever has gone, thank the heavens. Steven is so much better now. Thank you, Amy, but how have you been? How are you finding Gray Rock?"

"I like it," Amy answered. "Everyone is so good to me. I think I will like Peter and that he will make a good husband."

"Peter is a nice person," Gloria said, smiling. "He's really... nice."

"Do you know him well?" Amy asked. "I asked Drusilla when I arrived, and she said she tended to Peter because he was injured when she first got here. He had just been mugged. She said Peter was one of the first people to welcome her."

"Well..." Gloria tilted her head to the side. "Peter is my husband's friend. We have dinner together every other day, so I can say from the little I know that he is a good man. You have nothing to worry about, he is great."

There was something Amy wanted to ask Gloria, but she couldn't find the right words to say it. In fact, Amy wasn't even sure she had a question. All she knew was that it seemed Gloria was withholding information and trying to play it safe with her answers.

"All right, I'm back," Drusilla announced, stepping into the room. "Come on, Amy. Try on your dress, let's see you."

Excited, Amy rose to her feet, undressed, and tried on the dress Drusilla had set aside for her. It was a silk, cream-colored one, with a square-cut neck, puffy shoulders, long sleeves, and a bit of lace for a train. Mixed emotions coursed through Amy's body, as she stared into the mirror, and she was unsure of which one to feel.

"Oh, I just knew it!" Drusilla shrieked. "I feel like it's my wedding day all over again."

Gloria joined them by the mirror and examined the dress. Amy could see the sparkle in their eyes as the two women took their time, assessing her.

"Amy, you're gorgeous," Gloria said, running her hand over the dress. "Peter is going to forget how to breathe when he sees you walking down the aisle."

Amy stared at the dress in the mirror with quivering lips. "I should note that I've never received so many compliments in my entire life before. Thank you. You both really think I look pretty?"

"You're more than pretty," Gloria said.

"You're beautiful," Drusilla added. "Oh, if Carrie were here right now, she would be so happy to see you looking so wonderful."

Amy's grin slowly waned. "I wish my glasses didn't mar my appearance the way they do. I'd prefer to walk down the aisle without them but... I might trip and that would be so embarrassing."

"Nonsense. What are you saying?" Drusilla asked. "Your glasses do not change a thing about how you look."

"Absolutely. Knowing Peter, I'm certain he sees past the spectacles and only notices the light in your eyes."

Amy was quick to take note of the fact that Gloria claimed Peter was only a friend of her husband, yet she could say for certain what he was thinking. Why was she having these thoughts, these doubts? She brushed it off. Gloria probably said what she said to make Amy feel better. To put her at ease.

"Thank you," Amy said. "Really. This is one of the best days of my life. If I'm being honest. If there's anything, apart from Peter that makes me happy I made the decision to come here, it will be you, Drusilla, and you Gloria. You have no idea how much I craved friendships back in Virginia. Now, not only do I have a good man by my side, I have acquired friends too."

"Stop," Drusilla said, giving Amy a hug. "You're going to make me cry. I can't wait for you to become the most beautiful bride that there is."

"Will you be my matron of honor, Drusilla?" Amy asked.

Drusilla and Gloria grinned as they exchanged glances. "I'd be honored," Drusilla said.

Amy hugged them both, but why did she feel so worried? Everything was going well, better than she could have hoped for, and yet there was a seed of doubt, the worry that something was being kept from her. What was it?

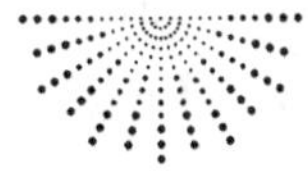

CHAPTER TWELVE

"A big day for you, Peter! Are you nervous?" Jamison asked.

Nervous was an understatement. Peter was sweating in places he didn't even know that he could sweat. He had seen Jamison and Eugene tie the knot, and he had been present. But he never imagined that on his own special day, he would be this nervous.

He sat in the chapel, waiting for his cue to stand at the altar. They had chosen to have a small wedding and only his friends, Jamison and Eugene and a few of the miners were present. It was the day Peter had been looking forward to for as long as he could recall.

"Why do I feel so nervous, Jamie?" Peter rasped. "Is this normal? I don't think this is normal. It can't be normal. It feels like someone is stirring my insides with a spoon. I mean, I feel hot, but cold inside. What is happening?"

Jamison chuckled and squeezed Peter's shoulders. "You're getting married. That's what's happening. It's only your nerves. Don't worry. I'm your best man, and it's my duty to assure you that everything will go perfectly. Once you have said your vows and the priest has pronounced you man and wife, all the tension will go. Trust me."

"If you say so." Peter let out a long breath.

"Well, if it isn't the groom who chose Jamison over me as his best man," Eugene said, joining them.

"Are you still whining about this?" Jamison asked him.

"Peter was my best man at my wedding," Eugene noted, taking his seat. "It's only normal that I expected him to ask me to be his best man. And yes, I am going to be petty about it."

"I can't have two," Peter said. "And you understand why I chose Jamison, Eugene, you're just choosing to taunt me about it."

"Well, seeing as you made it your duty once upon a time to frustrate me, I think I deserve to have some fun with this," Eugene said. "You don't look well, Peter. What's wrong?"

"He's nervous," Jamison explained.

"Ah, it's expected. You'll soon be fine. Once it's all over, you're going to feel just amazing."

"I'll leave you both to talk," Jamison said, rising to his feet.

Peter shut his eyes and leaned on the chair. He couldn't wait for the pastor to make the pronouncement that would, in turn, kickstart a life he had only dreamed of. Just thinking about holding Amy's hands in front of the altar made him smile to himself.

"This is the last time I'll be talking to you as a single man, Peter," Eugene said. "The next time we'll be speaking, you'll be married. Like Jamison and I."

"I can't wait," Peter said, glancing at him. "Do you recall our meeting with Carrie? The one where we told her that we wanted brides too?"

"Of course, I do. It seems like so long ago," Eugene said, staring at the altar. "That started everything for the both of us."

"I'm glad we both made that decision," Peter said. "Life before all of this had been so..."

"Plain? Unexciting? Draining?"

"Yes." Peter scoffed. "It had been all of those things. But look at us now."

Eugene turned to Peter. "Peter... about Gloria..."

Peter groaned in response. "Eugene, I'm not angry at you. I know you're about to apologize for taking her from me, but you don't have to do that every few months. I mean, come on. We've already been through this. I admit that I was hurt when Gloria left me for you, but that was because I was disappointed that things didn't work out for me. But there is no doubt that you and Gloria are a great match. Everyone is happy. I'm about to marry someone. And she is someone who, for the first time in my life, makes my heart skip beats when she smiles. I am happy with how things turned out."

"Me too," Eugene said. "I am even happier that you're finally finding your own woman to love."

Peter stretched his hand to Eugene. "Hopefully, we only have better days ahead."

Eugene smiled and shook his hand. "Amen to that."

When it was time for the ceremony to begin, Peter stood by the altar with Jamison behind him. He heard the doors of the chapel open first, but Peter didn't look in Amy's direction immediately. He waited until he had control of his emotions before lifting his head to see his bride.

"Oh, my," he whispered.

The excitement he felt at that moment was enough to cause his knees to buckle. Peter grinned at Amy as she walked down the aisle, smiling at him. They were staring into each other's eyes, lost in their own world. Peter didn't take another breath, neither did he take his eyes off Amy until she reached the altar and he took her hands into his.

"You look beautiful, Amy," he whispered. "Absolutely breathtaking."

Amy blushed. "Thank you. Drusilla was certain you'd love the dress," she whispered back.

"I wasn't talking about the dress. Well, the dress is indeed beautiful, but how could I notice the dress when I was lost in your eyes?"

Amy smiled in response and lowered her gaze. Soon after, the pastor cleared his throat, and the ceremony officially began. Peter was the first to say his vows to Amy, and he did so with so much pride. When it was Amy's turn, her voice quivered, and there were tears in her eyes.

"I now pronounce you man and wife," the pastor said. "You may kiss the bride."

Peter reached for Amy first and placed his hands on her face, cupping her cheeks. Gently, his lips found hers in a soft, slow kiss. Amy held on to his shirt tightly as she parted her lips to him. Just like Jamison had told him, the tension he felt earlier had dissipated, and Peter felt his heart leap with joy.

Amy was the first to break the kiss. She fell into Peter's arms and hugged him tightly as the congregation cheered for them.

And then there was a sudden loud bang. Was that a gunshot?

CHAPTER THIRTEEN

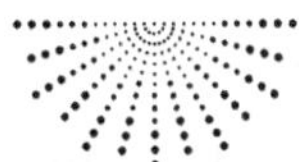

Peter recognized the gunshot and it caused him to instantly freeze. It was loud enough for him to be sure that he wasn't imagining it.

Instinctively, he pulled Amy behind him, guarding her with his body, just as a barrage of bullets came ripping into the church, sending everyone scattering in a state of chaos. Screams ripped through the air and people dived for cover.

"Get down, Amy!" he called as he tried to work out what was happening. Two men stood at the entrance, shooting. They wore Stetsons and had their faces covered, but inside he knew it was the gang of bandits. Would they ever be rid of them?

Amy covered her ears with her hands as she went down to the floor. She shut her eyes tightly. Her heart raced, faster than it had ever done before. Peter covered her with his body, and she could hear his heart beating too. In a strange way, she felt both terrified and comforted. He would know what to do. However, she had no idea what was going on. The screaming was loud, but the gun shots were louder.

"Peter," she whispered even though she knew he couldn't hear her. "What is happening?"

Amy could only hope that everyone was able to take cover when the bullets started flying. She hoped that no one was injured. The mere thought of someone dying at her wedding was something she didn't think she could live with.

Still, the most important questions on her mind were, was what was going on, who were these people, and why were they shooting up the church on her wedding day?

Mustering up all the courage she possibly could, Amy opened her eyes to scan the room. It was bedlam, people hiding everywhere. Gloria squatted behind an upturned pew, Carrie by her side bleeding...

"Oh, dear Lord," Amy said with a shuddering breath. "Carrie..."

Her blood chilled when she recalled Drusilla was heavily pregnant. Amy shifted, trying to find Drusilla, searching the church as much as she could, but to no avail. She caught a glimpse of Eugene pulling something out of a holster that was under his jacket. Amy watched him instead. Her eyes widened when she saw him pull out a pistol and begin to aim. *Why did he have a gun at her wedding?*

His first shot managed to hit one of the men shooting at him, but the man had his hand on the trigger when he went down. A bullet hit Eugene in return, striking him in the shoulder. His gun dropped from his hand and spun in her direction as he fell to the floor.

Gloria's scream was so loud, Amy had to cover her ears again. With tears in her eyes, Amy watched Gloria crawl to Eugene's side and press his wound with her hands.

"Eugene!"

Jamison's voice caught Amy's attention. She raised her head and finally found Drusilla in Jamison's arms. But from the expression on Drusilla's face, Amy could tell something was wrong, and she feared for the worst. Drusilla was sweating profusely as she labored for breath.

The baby was coming.

"Don't move, Amy," Peter told her. "Stay put behind this pew. Don't raise your head."

"No, Peter…" Amy said as she began to cry.

Without listening to what she wanted to say, Peter hurriedly picked up the gun and stood upright. He held the gun at arm's length with both hands, though it was only seconds, it felt like forever. Amy waited for him to be shot, praying that it wouldn't happen. She covered her ears as Peter pulled the trigger once, hitting one of the shooters straight in the chest. He moved his hands quickly to his left and fired another shot. Amy peered over the pew and saw the man drop to the floor. Peter was good at this, he would keep them safe, he did not miss.

Amy had dropped behind the pew, breathing heavily but she had to look and lifted her head to see one of the men aim at Peter.

She was about to scream when she saw the man pull the trigger twice. Her heart froze in her chest, but nothing happened! He was out of bullets.

With a scream, the man threw the gun to the ground and charged for Peter. Amy had her heart in her mouth when he rammed into Peter, sending them both to the ground, and sending the gun flying out of Peter's grip.

Amy screamed and immediately sprung to her feet. She had risen so quickly that her glasses fell from her face and shattered on the ground.

"Let my husband go!" she screeched, unable to make out the man's face.

Peter kicked the man in the groin and rose to his feet. The man struggled at first, but he was able to stand up too.

The shooting had stopped, and at that moment, she could hear grunts and punches being thrown. It seemed as though the shooters had run out of bullets and were now trying to fight their way through this.

But Peter was her concern. Even without her glasses, Amy could still see him struggling with the man.

"Happy married life, Peter," the man said, cackling.

"I'll make you pay for this, Mitch Stokes," Peter rasped.

The man Peter had called Mitch reached behind him and pulled out a knife. He reached for Peter and swung his knife at his face, aiming for his neck but Peter swerved, avoiding the blade. Mitch kept swinging, trying to land one good strike on Peter, but was unable to do so. Peter seemed to be waiting for his own opening, and when he found it, he charged for Mitch, grabbing the man by the waist with a force that sent them both to the ground.

"The baby is coming!" Amy heard Drusilla scream.

"What do I do?" Amy whispered as she began to panic.

It seemed as though Mitch had the advantage now. He had found his way on top of Peter and tried to subdue him. Peter made sure to hold Mitch's wrist at arm's length, keeping the knife as far away from him as possible. But Mitch's hand was inching closer and closer to Peter's face. The knife was only a few inches away from cutting her husband.

"Peter!" Amy yelled, and she took off her shoe and struck Mitch's head.

Her action gave Peter the opening he needed.

Mitch grunted and was temporarily distracted by the pain. Peter grabbed Mitch and threw him off his body. It gave Peter time to find his footing, but as they were about to charge for each other again, another gunshot caused everyone to freeze.

CHAPTER FOURTEEN

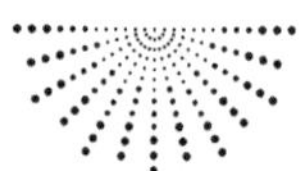

"On your feet!"

Amy dropped to the ground and peered over the pew. Relief washed over her, a man in a sheriff's uniform and some other armed men walked into the church.

She didn't know if it was over, but she was glad that the sheriff had his gun pointed at Mitch, the man that was trying to hurt Peter. Amy couldn't think straight. She had never been this scared in her entire life.

"Jamie!"

The sound of Drusilla screaming shook Amy back to reality. She crawled over to Drusilla's side at the edge of the room. Amy took Drusilla's hand into hers and caressed it.

"Breathe, Drusilla. It's only the shock. It's not yet time to give birth to your little bundle of blessing," Amy told her. "Breathe."

"Amy, I really feel like it's time," Drusilla groaned. "The baby's coming, I can feel it."

"Breathe," Amy said, panting. "Try to take deep breaths."

"My water broke," Drusilla announced. "It's coming. But it's too early. What do I do?"

If the water truly broke, then Drusilla was right. She had every right to be worried. But Drusilla was only seven months pregnant. Having the baby so early was going to put the little one in danger.

"I'm here," Jamison said, joining them. "It's going to be fine. I've sent for the doctor and he'll be here shortly. I won't leave your side."

Amy scanned the room, noticing that Carrie was all alone in the middle of the chapel. She was bleeding from her leg and attempting to use a ripped length of cloth to bind the wound.

"Someone needs to be with Carrie," Drusilla said, grunting. "Go, Jamie. Amy is here with me."

"No, I'll go," Amy volunteered. "Jamison, you stay here with Drusilla. If the pain doesn't subside soon, we might have to deliver the baby before the physician gets here. I don't know much, but I should be able to do it. I'll go check on Carrie and see how bad her injury is first."

"Thank you," Jamison said.

Amy nodded and crawled over to Carrie's side. The sheriff and his men were still trying to subdue Mitch and his men, but they weren't making it easy for them. Amy looked away and continued making her way across to Carrie. As long as Peter was out of Mitch's reach, she was fine.

"You're only making this more difficult than it needs to be," Amy heard the sheriff say. "All your men will be rounded up. You can choose to come with us quietly, or we will be forced to shoot."

"Carrie, are you all right?" Amy asked. She took the length of cloth from her hand and assessed the wound. "Were you shot?"

Carrie forced a smile. "No. This happened when I fell. I don't think it's deep, but it's bleeding a lot."

"Oh, Carrie. I'm so sorry," Amy said with a quaking voice. "Jamison says the doctor will be here shortly. I'll stop the bleeding, if I can, before then. Do you know what cut you?"

"I'm not sure. I think it was the sharp edge of one of these pews caused when a bullet hit them," Carrie answered. "You're not to blame, Amy. There's no need to apologize. The sheriff is here now, and I'm sure he has everything under control."

"Who are these men?" Amy asked, binding Carrie's wound as tightly as she could. "It doesn't look like they came here to steal. I mean, who steals from a wedding? Earlier, Peter called one of them by his name. It looks as if they came here with the intent to kill all of us. I don't understand it."

Carrie sighed. "These men have been thorns in our flesh for as long as I can recall. We thought we had got rid of them twice, but here they are again. Hopefully, this is the last of them. Mitch was someone called Albie's, right-hand man. If Albie and Mitch are both gone, perhaps, we will finally have some peace."

"Albie?" Amy mumbled.

"Are you hurt anywhere, Amy?" Carrie asked her.

Amy shook her head. "No, I'm not. I'm fine. Peter protected me. Thankfully, he's not hurt either. I think. I might need to check. I should have checked him for injuries first. I didn't."

Amy instinctively rose to her feet to check for Peter. She had rushed to Drusilla's side before even checking to see if Peter was all right. What if he was injured and bleeding? He would have expected her to check on him first. But she didn't.

"Go to him," Carrie said to her. "I'm sure he's fine, but you can go to him."

"Are you sure, Carrie? You're bleeding too."

"I'm all right. You bound my wound tighter than I could. I'll be fine. Go to him."

Amy nodded and ran over to Peter's side. The sheriff had finally been able to subdue Mitch and they were forcing him to the ground to shackle his hands. Amy placed both hands on Peter's arms and examined him.

"Are you all right?" she asked. "Are you hurt anywhere? I'm sorry, Drusilla was screaming and I..."

"No, Amy, I'm glad you went to check on the others," Peter said. "I'm completely fine. It's all right. Are you hurt?"

"I'm fine," Amy said. "I was so scared, Peter. I thought he was going to really hurt you."

Peter smiled and cupped her face. "Well, your shoe did most of the work for me. If you hadn't hit him in his head, I don't know what might have happened."

Amy giggled. "I'm glad you're all right."

"Me too," Peter whispered and hugged her.

While his men took care of Mitch, the sheriff approached them, tucking his gun away. "I'm sorry about what happened here, Peter."

Peter stood in front of Amy and placed both hands on his hips. "How did you know to come here, Sheriff Hill?"

"Well, my men and I have had out eyes on Mitch for a while. We heard he was in the next town, so I had men stationed at the entrance of the town, and in the woods, to make sure we knew when they'd re-enter Gray Rock. I sensed that they would do something like this after we arrested Albie Oleson several months ago. I'm sorry we didn't arrive sooner. Thankfully, this is the last of the surviving members of Albie's gang."

"I truly hope so, Sheriff," Peter said. "All I want is for Mitch and his gang members to leave us alone. They have done us enough damage as it is."

The sheriff nodded. "This is the last of them. Don't worry. I'll make sure they are gone for a long time."

Amy met Mitch's gaze as the men dragged him away. Blood trickled down his face, from the wound she had inflicted on him. His stare turned into a glare, and Mitch smirked at her.

"How can you be happy as his second option?" Mitch yelled as he was being carted away. "If things went according to Peter's plan, he'd rather be married to Gloria Tompkins but she rejected him and chose the other one."

Hurt tore through her for she knew this was true. It made sense and was why she had felt unsure. Her gut was right after all.

Peter turned to her, and even without her glasses, she could see the look on his face. Peter tried to reach for her hand, but Amy brushed it away and stormed over to Drusilla.

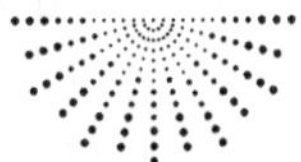

CHAPTER FIFTEEN

"We have to do this, Drusilla. You need to be ready. The baby is coming."

Peter scanned the room, dazed at how the church had now become a make-shift clinic. Carrie was injured, but luckily, her wound was not too severe and it was easy to stop the bleeding. She was seated in the fourth row, unable to move around.

Gloria was by Eugene's side, sobbing. Eugene had been shot in the shoulder and was still bleeding, despite them trying to stop the blood. Steven was in tears too and holding Eugene's other arm tightly.

Amy was by Drusilla's side. The baby was coming, she was sure of it. They were all very scared for the baby. It wasn't time for the little one to be born but there was nothing they could do to stop it.

Jamison held Drusilla's hand tightly as she winced and writhed in pain. Amy stood on Drusilla's other side. She was trying to calm Drusilla but it wasn't working.

Peter stood in the middle of the room. The sheriff had left with the last of Albie's gang a while ago, and the people that remained in the church after the shooting were still gathering themselves and trying to come to terms with what happened.

"What's Drusilla going to do?" Lenard, one of the miners present asked. "It looks like she might have to birth her baby without a doctor or midwife present."

Peter glanced at Lenard. "Can you please go and fetch the doctor? I think Jamison has already sent for someone, but I need him to hurry up."

"On it," Lenard said and scurried out of the church.

Almost everyone had left. Only Carrie, the Tompkins, the McCord's, and the Quinn's remained.

"Oh, I don't think I can do this for much longer!" Drusilla screamed and gritted her teeth. Her screams rang out once more as another contraction hit her.

Peter walked over to their side and joined them on the floor. Jamison had placed a white sheet underneath Drusilla and there was a bag beneath her head. Drusilla was sweating so much, and she was panting. Things did not look good.

"Is there any way I can help?" Peter asked, squatting by Amy's side. "Tell me what to do."

"We need to deliver the baby ourselves," Amy stated, avoiding eye contact with him. "We can't wait for the doctor. Drusilla needs to push now before she loses any more strength."

"No, make it stop," Drusilla screamed.

"It will," Amy said, "you have to push."

"I can't," she screamed and lay back as the pain eased.

"What do you need me to do?" Peter asked. "Can you deliver the baby, Amy?"

Amy nodded in response.

"Your glasses," Peter noted. "Amy, you don't have your glasses, are you certain that you can..."

"I can see good enough for this," Amy snapped. "If you want to help, you need to get some hot water in a big bowl, and some towels. I'm going to try and do this as safely as I can, but there are risks."

Drusilla gripped Amy's sleeve and squeezed tightly. "Amy, please do something. It hurts too much."

"Have you delivered a baby before, Amy?" Jamison asked. "Can you help her?"

"I've assisted in births twice," Amy answered. "I know what I'm doing, but I'm afraid we don't have everything I need to safely deliver this baby. But we will make do with what we have. Drusilla is going to need some privacy."

"Everyone else has left," Peter answered. "Carrie is tending to her wounds, and Gloria is trying to stop Eugene's bleeding until the doctor arrives. I'll go fetch what you asked for immediately."

Peter quickly rose to his feet and made his way to the back of the church. He knew the place well enough to remember that there was a stove in the kitchen beside the living quarters. Peter ran over there and was quick to find a kettle.

After running around for what seemed like forever, he finally got the items Amy needed. Carefully, he hurried back to her side.

Drusilla appeared weaker now. She could barely keep both eyes open for any length of time.

"Drusilla, you cannot fall asleep," Amy said to her. "In a few minutes, I'll need you to push."

"I don't think I can," Drusilla replied, almost in a whisper. "I can't... I can't bear it again and I feel so tired."

"Honey, you have to try," Jamison said. "For the baby's sake."

"All I need you to do is push until I get a glimpse of the baby's head. Then, I'll ask you to stop pushing as I gently guide the shoulders of the baby out. I need you to trust me and push as hard as you can."

"I'll give you some privacy," Peter said and rose to his feet.

Drusilla's screams filled the church as Peter walked away from them. He felt sorry for her, and for Jamison who was clearly terrified. Anger made him clench his fists. Why did this happen? This was not the plan. They had a little over a month before they had to prepare for the arrival of the little one. Now, all of a sudden, their world had been turned upside down and Drusilla had to birth her child early and in such awful conditions. Peter could only pray that the baby was delivered safe and sound.

He sat at a pew and then dropped to his knees. If he was going to pray, he guessed he was in the right place.

* * *

"This is not a great way to end your wedding," Carrie said with a sigh.

Peter had finished his prayer and came to sit by her side. "I fear for the baby, for both of them."

"Me too," Carrie said. "I should be there with her, but Drusilla needs her space right now, and Amy looks like she has it under control. Oh, Dear Lord. I wouldn't be able to bear it if anything happened to that child."

Peter raised his head and placed his hand on Carrie's. "How do you feel right now?"

Carrie drew in a raggedy breath. "Well, the room is spinning, and it's difficult to move my leg, but other than that, I'm fine. I cannot imagine what Gloria is going through right now. Eugene doesn't look too well, and the doctor is still not here, he must have been out on a call."

Peter diverted his gaze to Eugene and Gloria. There was nothing he could do for them at that moment. Eugene looked like he was falling asleep, his lips were blue and his eyes kept closing.

"Gloria, how is he?" Peter called across to her. "He can't fall asleep."

"I'm trying," Gloria said. "I think the bleeding has stopped but I don't want to take the cloth off to check. But he keeps closing his eyes, even when I talk to him. He's lost so much blood, Peter."

"Just keep the pressure on it, and don't take the cloth off," Peter said to her. "Lenard went to fetch the doctor, and he should be here any minute now. Hang on."

"I will," Gloria managed to say. "Eugene, come on. Keep your eyes open."

"Why does this always happen to us, Peter?" Carrie asked. "First, it was you. They nearly killed you just because they wanted to rob you. Then, it was Drusilla. They took her money, chased her, and if it wasn't for Jamison and Eugene, Lord knows what they might have done to her. Then, it was Gloria. The poor lady and her son had just arrived in this town. But Albie kidnapped her, and almost took her away. Now this. This could have ended worse than it did."

Peter nodded. "I agree. I think they didn't come with enough bullets, and they were shooting blindly. If they had known what they were doing... it's a miracle we're sitting here talking to each other. Those men were hell bent on killing us. The rage in Mitch's eyes when he charged me... I couldn't understand it. I never offended this man. If anything, he offended me. We only took back our town from the menaces that plagued it, and they chose to retaliate like this. They chose to hunt us."

"I wonder if we have truly seen the last of them," Carrie said. "I don't want to live out the rest of my life always looking over my shoulder."

"I reckon we have," Peter said. "With Albie and Mitch gone, the gang is done for. Plus, the sheriff has them all in custody. As long they go to prison and pay for their crimes, we can sleep peacefully at night."

Just as Carrie and Peter held hands to comfort each other, the sound of a baby crying caused them both to gasp and rise to their feet.

"It's a girl," Amy announced.

CHAPTER SIXTEEN

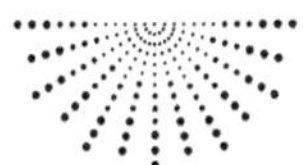

"The baby looks older than seven months. It is possible that you were off with the date of conception." Amy asked.

"We could have been, we've been married long enough but I just thought I knew when I was pregnant," Drusilla said.

Peter watched Carrie gather the newborn into her arms with tears in her eyes. Amy had done it. She had delivered the baby like she said she would. Both mother and baby were safe and sound. Drusilla had come through the birth well, but she was exhausted. What with the birth and the shock from the attack, she was too weak to keep her eyes open.

After greeting his newborn baby, Jamison handed her over to Carrie, and held on to Drusilla tightly.

Soon after, the doctor arrived with an assistant, and they instantly got to work. Lenard had told him that Drusilla was in labor, so he checked on her first. His assistant, John Parker, got to work on Eugene. He managed to stop the bleeding, and was now inspecting the wound.

"Luckily, the bullet went in, and straight out without hitting anything major," John said. "I need to clean the wound, and stitch him up. I can do some of that here, but once I'm sure he's out of danger, we will have to move him to a better location."

"Thank you," Gloria said.

Thankfully, Drusilla was out of danger too. Together with Amy, the doctor checked her over, and checked on the baby. Peter stood by Amy's side, watching her work with a serious look on her face. He wanted to tell her that he was proud of her, but she was too busy and he hated to disturb her. He didn't know how she would react, was she still angry with him?

"You did good, Jamie," Peter said to his friend, patting him on the shoulder. "I know this must have been really difficult for you, but you managed to push through. You did well."

"Peter, I never want to go through this again," Jamison said, he was out of breath. "I thought the fear was going to kill me. These men were still shooting when Drusilla went into labor, and in that moment, the gunshots didn't scare me half as much as seeing Drusilla's water break did."

"Believe me, I understand," Peter replied. "The sheriff took Mitch away. They won't bother us again."

"Mitch?" Jamison asked. "Mitch Stokes?"

Peter nodded. "The very one. Albie's right-hand man."

Jamison shut his eyes and sighed. "We should have known. Of course, they came for revenge."

"I think deep down we knew but we let our guard down," Peter said. "It's been months. We knew Albie's gang was still out there, but we just didn't imagine they would be evil enough to shoot at us at a wedding."

"Did the sheriff round up all of them?" Jamison asked.

"I think so. But it doesn't matter. With Albie and Mitch gone, it's over. There's little any of them could do without the backing of their leaders."

"So, it's all over?"

Peter sighed. "I hope so."

"How's Carrie?" Jamison sniffed. "I checked on her earlier, when the shooting had stopped, but Drusilla needed me."

"Her bleeding has stopped, you don't have to worry," Peter told him. "They are treating Eugene right now. He doesn't look too well, but the doctor says he'll recover."

"Thank goodness," Jamison sighed.

Amy rose to her feet, done with the work she had to do for Drusilla. That was Peter's opening to talk to her. After what Mitch had said earlier, he could tell that something was off. Although the traumatic events that happened at their wedding was enough to steal her smile, Amy was overly serious. She had not really looked at him since they said their vows. She barely responded when he spoke to her, and seeing how she had yanked her hand away from his grip after Mitch spat his rubbish, there was no denying that she was taking it badly.

"Amy," Peter called her, stopping her in her tracks. He stood in front of her, and cleared his throat. "Hey."

"I have to check on Carrie."

There was definitely something wrong. She spoke without looking at him, and her eyes were cold. This wasn't the Amy that had examined him with concern a short while ago.

"You were amazing. I don't know what we would have done if you weren't here."

Amy responded by nodding, and proceeded to walk around Peter.

"Wait," Peter said, grabbing her by the arm. "Amy, what's wrong? You won't look at me and I'm trying to talk to you, but you're avoiding me. Did I do something wrong?"

"You really don't know what's wrong?" Amy asked, still avoiding his gaze. "I need to check on Carrie. She lost a lot of blood."

Amy walked away from Peter, and like she said, she went to Carrie's side and checked her wound. Peter was dumbfounded. Mitch had said hurtful things, but how in the world was he going to clear the air if she wouldn't talk to him?

After confirming that Jamison and Drusilla were going to be all right, Peter joined Gloria and Eugene. Thankfully, Eugene was awake now, and although he was still pale, it looked like he was out of danger.

"How are you, my friend?" Peter asked him. "You must be in a lot of pain."

"It hurts so much," Eugene said, chuckling. "But I think I'll survive. That's if the painful stitching doesn't kill me."

"Don't joke about these things," Gloria said to Eugene. "You gave us quite a scare. I kept calling your name but it seemed like you weren't here. Do you know how scared I was?"

"I can only imagine," Eugene said. "I'm sorry. I didn't mean to scare you. But I'm grateful that I'm still here. I couldn't bear the thought of not seeing your beautiful face ever again."

"Does it still hurt, Eugene?" Steven asked, fixing a curious gaze on him.

Eugene nodded in response. "But only a bit. A hug from you will fix it though."

Peter couldn't help but smile as Steven wrapped his small hands around Eugene and embraced him. It looked like all that was left was for them to recover from the shock.

"I need to get back to Amy," Peter said.

"I just saw her leave. She's gone," Eugene said. "She just left with Jamison, Carrie and Drusilla. Didn't she tell you?"

Peter rose to his feet swiftly and scanned the empty church. Amy hadn't told him that she was leaving. Her action only proved Peter right. She was upset.

Very upset with him. A touch of fear traced a finger down his spine. Could he win her back?

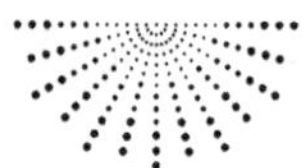

"Peter, will you please help Eugene into the wagon?"

For a moment, Peter hesitated. His first instinct was to go after Amy, and take her with him. They had just tied the knot, she should be by his side. But if Amy was truly angry like he thought, then perhaps, it was a good idea to let her go for now and hopefully, she would cool off. He didn't want to imagine that she had taken Mitch's words that seriously. Amy must know that he only said it to spite her.

Together with Gloria, Peter helped get Eugene into the wagon, and they made their way to his home together with the doctor. As they rode to the house, Peter couldn't get Amy's angry face out of his head. He couldn't bear the thought of upsetting her on their wedding day.

"What do I do?" he mumbled, running his fingers through his hair.

"I heard what Mitch said," Eugene said, as if he had read Peter's mind. "Is that the reason you're so worked up?"

Peter nodded. "He said it to spite her, Eugene, but I'm afraid Amy took his words to heart. She's angry. I have no idea what to do. Everything has been turned upside down."

"Well, you should get too worked up," Eugene said. "Did you not tell Amy about Gloria during the weeks that you both courted?"

"I didn't. We could talk about it anytime. It's not that serious now, is it?" Peter asked. "I mean, it's not serious enough to make her angry."

Eugene shook his head and turned to Gloria. "Did you tell her?"

"I didn't," Gloria admitted. "I didn't think it was my place to talk about it."

"How did you both expect Amy to react?" Eugene asked and groaned. "Did you hear what Mitch said to her? I heard it, and I was angry on her behalf. She didn't deserve to hear those words, Peter. Not on her wedding day. This could have been avoided, if you had explained to her and had assured her of her place from the start."

"Amy knows that I love her," Peter said. "I think she's just angry that I didn't tell her."

"You should be by her side right now," Eugene said. "I'm grateful that you're helping me, but right now, Amy needs you. The sooner you sort out this mess, the better. If you let it linger, she will stay angry. I mean, she has no idea what you and Gloria had in the past, don't let her get ideas in her head and make more of it than there was."

"Ideas?" Peter repeated. "I really don't want to believe that this is a big deal. I mean, Amy won't believe the words of a criminal over me. She trusts me."

"Peter, Eugene is right. You should be by Amy's side right now, even if she's refusing to talk to you," Gloria said. "Be there for her, and then talk about what happened today when you have the chance. Just like Eugene said, the sooner you do it, the better.

Peter leaned back and sighed. He had to figure out a way to talk to Amy, that didn't involve bringing up what

Mitch had said. Although Eugene made it clear that Amy was angry for that particular reason, Peter still didn't want to believe that it was serious. She was angry with him, but it was nothing an explanation wouldn't fix.

When they reached Eugene's home, the doctor finished dressing the wound and was about to take his leave.

"You have to clean the area every day," he said to Gloria as they strolled to the door. "It must not get infected. If he starts to run a fever, don't panic. It's normal. But if the fever persists, then you must send for me immediately. Also, monitor the color of the wound. If it starts to turn any other color aside raw pink, or the healthy subtle darker color when it starts to heal, send for me. I'll come by in three days to check the stitches."

"Thank you," Gloria said.

"Are you're sure you know how to dress his wound?"

"I am," Gloria answered. "Thank you, Doctor Richards."

"It's not a problem," he said. "Eugene is going to be in a lot of pain for the next few days. Don't worry, he will make a slow, but full recovery. Make sure he eats, and takes opium. Remember all the signs I asked you to look out for."

"I will," Gloria said. She shut the door behind her once the doctor was gone and collapsed on the wall.

"It'll be all right," Peter told her. "Just make sure you call the doctor at any slight questionable change. I'll be back tomorrow to check on him."

Gloria nodded. "Thank you, Peter. I'm sorry for taking up so much of your time. You should go and apologize to Amy. I need to go back to Eugene's side."

"I will," Peter said, taking his leave.

"Oh, and Peter." Gloria stopped him in his tracks. "Make things right with her. Amy is a wonderful young lady who doesn't deserve to think of herself as a replacement like Mitch said."

Peter let out a soft breath. The situation seemed to be more serious than he thought it was. Why had everyone seen this but him?

CHAPTER EIGHTEEN

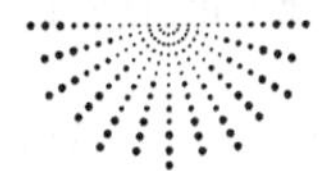

Once Peter arrived at the McCord house, he found Carrie first, seated in the living room, groaning in pain. He took his seat by her side, feeling sorry for her. A part of him felt guilty for all that had happened. It was at his wedding after all. If he hadn't gathered them all in the same place, none of this would have happened.

"Don't do that, Peter," Carrie said, groaning as she set her foot down.

"Do what?" Peter asked, lifting his head so their gazes met.

"Blame yourself," Carrie said. "I know you, more than you know yourself. I've watched you for years. I know that face. You're currently soaking in all of the blame for all that happened. I don't want you to do that. This has nothing to do with you."

"It was my wedding, Carrie," Peter said quietly. "I gathered you all. If it wasn't for me, this wouldn't have taken place."

Carrie sucked in a breath. "What did I just ask you not to do?"

"It's too much," Peter continued. "You, Drusilla and the baby, Eugene... I can't help but think that it could have been a lot worse."

"But it wasn't."

"But it could have been."

"Would you not blame yourself for what could have been, and be thankful that we are all still alive? You were bound to marry eventually. No matter the day, they must have known that you had found a bride. This isn't on you. If anyone is to take blame for anything, then it should be those evil men."

"I'm sorry you have to suffer like this, Carrie."

Carrie winked at him. "A few battle scars, I can take it," she teased. "I'll heal. The doctor just left not too long ago. The baby is frail, but she will survive. Drusilla is resting comfortably with Jamison by her side. All seems to be well. We should be glad that these men that have long plagued our lives have met their end. Don't dwell too much on this."

Just then, Jamison walked into the living room and crashed on the sofa. "Drusilla has fallen asleep," he announced.

"Did the doctor say anything?" Peter asked him.

"She needs to rest. Delivering our baby took its toll on her, she lost blood, and her energy is completely drained. He recommended that she stays in bed for about two days. Then he will be back to check on her again. As for our baby, we have to be extra careful with her. But Amy was right. She wasn't seven months. Drusilla and I were off by a month, maybe a bit more. She was still born early, but not that early."

"Thank goodness for that," Peter said with a sigh. "I'm sorry, Jamie. I'm so sorry for everything."

"Don't do that, Peter. You'll just make it worse," Jamison said.

"I already told him," Carrie said.

"This isn't your fault in anyway," Jamison continued. "I don't want us feeling sorry for ourselves. They tried to bring us down, but we won. We were able to overcome them. Soon, we will all recover from this. You'll see."

Peter nodded and sighed. He scanned the room, about to ask where Amy was when she walked out of the kitchen and into the living room. She had a new pair of glasses on her face. Peter met her gaze and smiled but in return, Amy walked out of the house.

"I'll be back," Peter said to Carrie and Jamison. "I need to talk to my wife."

With that, he made his way out of the house and joined Amy in the yard. She stood by the fence, in the spot where they had first had a long conversation.

Without saying a word, Peter tiptoed over to her side. He reached Amy and hugged her from behind. He thought she'd pry him away from her body, but Amy just stood still.

"I see you have new glasses," he said.

"They're an old pair."

"It's good that you had them. We should talk."

Amy remained silent, even after moments had passed since Peter made the remark. Peter dropped his hands to the side and stood in front of Amy.

"Amy, I'm sorry for the bloodshed that happened at our wedding," Peter started. "If I had known that something like this would happen, I would have done everything in my power to prevent it. I'm sorry you had to go through such a trauma. I assure you that it will never happen again."

"That's over and done. I don't care about that. You're talking about everything else, Peter," Amy finally said. "Everything other than what I want to hear from you. The fact that you are choosing to brush past what that man said to me only makes things worse. It only proves his point."

"I'm sorry for what Mitch said to you," Peter apologized. "I should have told you right from the start, but thinking that you're angry with me scares me. You must not let what he said get to you."

"Why not?"

"Amy..."

"You're not denying it," Amy continued. "Instead, you're avoiding telling me about it."

"You're already annoyed, I didn't know how to bring it up," Peter said. "I'm sorry. What Mitch said can be grossly misinterpreted. That's not what happened. The way he said it was wrong. I don't want you dwelling on something that doesn't matter."

"Why? I think I have a right to dwell on this, Peter. You and Gloria intentionally hid the fact that you had courted, from me. If that is truly not what happened, then why didn't you tell me about it, and why are you avoiding the subject now?"

Peter felt a panic clawing inside of him; he had to explain but the words would not seem to come. "I know how it sounded to you, but I need you to relax, and let me explain. Please."

Amy crossed her arms. "Are you truly where you want to be, Peter?"

Peter threw his hands in the air. "What does that mean?"

"You know what I mean."

"I don't. I really don't. Yes, I am where I want to be. You're speaking as if I have been unfaithful with you. This is all just a misunderstanding. What Mitch said shouldn't affect you this way."

"Then make me believe you," Amy demanded, her eyes were wild and filled with tears. "Tell me what I need to know."

CHAPTER NINETEEN

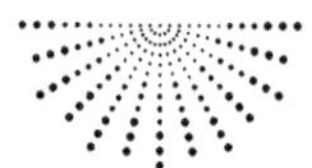

$\mathcal{P}$eter took a big breath and closed his eyes. He had to get this right, there was nothing to hide, but Amy had to understand that. He let the breath out and opened his eyes. "About... eight months ago, Gloria arrived in Gray Rock as my intended. I welcomed her, and she lived in my home with Steven, while I slept in the barn. We were getting to know each other, because we were soon to be married. But things didn't work out as we thought they would. Gloria was growing more attached to Eugene than to me because they had more in common. Unlike us. So, we came to an understanding, and she married Eugene instead of me."

Amy crossed her arms. "Peter, I asked you before if you had ever been in love!"

"I wasn't in love," Peter said. "That's what I'm trying to explain to you. We weren't in love, Amy. Gloria and I had very different interests. I admit that we got off to a great start at first, but it didn't last. I told you, I don't want a loveless marriage."

Amy was trying hard not to be hurt by something she couldn't change, but she couldn't help it. Peter was her first everything. Her first relationship, her first kiss, and the man she married. It hurt that he didn't tell her he had been engaged to Gloria, a woman Amy was now acquainted with. Why did the both of them hide the fact that they had been together once, unless in fact, there were lingering feelings.

"Amy," Peter said softly and reached for her face.

Amy turned away from his touch. "Don't, Peter. I need to think."

"Gloria belongs to Eugene now," he continued. "They are happy together. Whatever it is that was between Gloria and I ended seven months ago. We are friends now, and we understand each other. We were never meant to be."

"That's not my point," Amy said. "Am I not simply your second choice? If Gloria hadn't chosen Eugene over you, would you not be married to her right now?"

"Second choice?" Peter questioned. "Amy, don't think like that. Yes, there was a time when I wanted to marry Gloria. We were already making plans, but..."

Amy scoffed and turned away. He had just proven her point. Peter didn't send for her because he wanted her as a wife, he sent for her because he needed a replacement and she was the one that fit into the role.

As she turned to walk away, Peter grabbed her by the arm. "Amy, don't let something like this get to you. Please. I wanted a wife and a family. Gloria couldn't give me that. So, I turned to Carrie in search of a new bride."

"Peter, this just proves my point," Amy said with a quivering voice. "I wasn't your first choice, or a choice you made because you had come to like me through our many letters. I was a second choice. One to fulfil the needs your first choice couldn't give you. Don't you understand? I mean, isn't that why you didn't tell me? Isn't that the reason you kept it a secret from me?"

"I wasn't keeping it a secret," Peter said, for he truly hadn't been.

"Then why didn't you, or Gloria tell me?" Amy asked. "You knew this would happen. That's why you hid it."

"That's not true," Peter said. "You know that's not true, Amy. If I didn't love you, I wouldn't have asked you to marry me. I fell for you in such a short span of time. That's the truth, and I can prove it to you. If you give me a second chance. Besides, we're married, Amy. Can't we just give this a try? If you let me, I will prove it to you that I love you and only you."

"Peter, you don't understand why I'm annoyed. It will take more than your sweet words to prove anything to me. I'm not angry that you have courted in the past. I'm angry that you didn't think it was important enough to tell me. I'm angry that you don't realize you only sent for me as a second option, when you have been nothing but my first. Do you really think words will be enough to prove to me that I'm wrong?"

"Well, what do you want me to do?" Peter asked. "Tell me. I will do anything. I understand why you might be angry about this. But it is in the past, Amy."

"It's not in the past. It happened seven months ago," Amy said.

"Amy, I'm asking you not to see it like that," Peter said, taking her hands into his. "Why would you listen to what someone like Mitch said out of spite? You hit his head with your shoe, he was angry, and he wanted to hurt you back. Don't listen to him. Listen to me. I'm your husband, and I'm telling you that I love you. I don't want to be with anyone else."

"That's not..." Amy swallowed her words and pried her hands away from Peter's grasp. "Goodnight, Peter. I'll stay with Carrie and Drusilla for the meantime. Carrie is hurt, and Drusilla just put to bed. Seeing how Eugene got hurt too, he'll need Gloria by his side. I'll have to take care of Drusilla and Carrie while they recuperate."

"Amy..."

"We cannot do this now, Peter," Amy said. "Not when your friends are hurt."

Peter wanted to say something in response but he didn't. He lowered his head instead and nodded. "All right. I'll constantly check on Eugene until he recovers. But, Amy. You know I love you?"

Amy didn't respond. She walked away from Peter and made her way into the house without glancing back at him, even though she really wanted to. Amy couldn't tell if it was jealousy, heartbreak, or annoyance she felt. But whatever it was, it made her eyes water and her heart ache. She really wanted to cry, but there was too much going on. She couldn't think of herself in that moment.

CHAPTER TWENTY

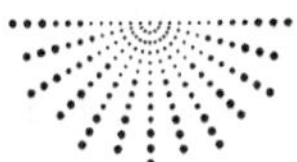

A FEW WEEKS LATER...

Peter made sure the lid on the pot was shut tightly before stuffing it into a bag. He had spent all morning making chicken soup, and finally, he was done, and ready to deliver one pot to Jamison and those with him, and one to Eugene and Gloria.

Two weeks had passed after the unfortunate incident at the church. Two weeks had passed since his wedding. Sadly, it didn't even seem as though he was married. His wife, Amy, barely met his gaze whenever he went over to Carrie's home to visit. The familiar feeling of heartbreak and loneliness had crept back into his heart. Perhaps he was destined to be unhappy, after all.

Strangely, he could now understand why Amy was upset. At first, Peter couldn't wrap his head around the reason for her anger. He had thought that if he apologized two or three times, she would forgive him, and they would move on. But that wasn't the case. It was only after he talked to Jamison about it, that Peter realized what he did that was so wrong.

It wasn't only about him. According to Jamison, Amy had come to love him too. But the realization that she wouldn't even be in Gray Rock at all, if Gloria hadn't rejected him broke her heart. Their love was built on the fact that Peter needed to find someone to take Gloria's place. Not only did Peter send for her as a second choice, but he didn't tell her about it. Amy had to hear it from Mitch. Even though Peter didn't see it in that light, Amy did, and she was not happy about it.

Jamison's advice to Peter had been to let Amy come to him. She was hurt now, but she couldn't be hurt forever. Sooner or later, they would come to a compromise. She couldn't stay angry at him for long.

Peter strolled over to Carrie's house with lunch in his hand. The past two weeks had been both stressful and tasking for him. Peter had to divide his time between the McCord's house, and the Tompkins's. He brought food for Jamison, Drusilla, Carrie and Amy, and he also had to visit Eugene to check on his injured friend.

Thankfully, everyone was making a good recovery. Eugene still couldn't move as much as he liked, but he was better than he was two weeks ago. Drusilla and the baby were doing well and they seemed to be out of danger.

"Good morning, Carrie," Peter greeted her on the porch. "You seem to be able to move around better these days. I'm glad to see it."

"Peter," Carrie beamed. "How are you, my darling?"

"I'm well," he answered, leaning on the pillar. "How are you, Carrie. How's your leg? Does it still hurt to walk?"

"A little," Carrie answered. "But I'm getting by just fine. Still limping, but the swelling has gone down. I think I'll be much better in a couple of days."

"And the baby?" he asked. "Drusilla?"

"They are fine," Carrie answered. "They gave us quite a scare, didn't they? The doctor came to check on them yesterday and he said they're doing great. There's no need to worry."

"And Amy?" Peter asked, staring at the ground. "Is she still very angry with me?"

Carrie sighed. "Honestly, I don't know, Peter. She doesn't want to talk about it and it would be harsh to make her when she's so busy taking care of the baby with Drusilla. But don't think about it too much, Peter. Amy is your wife now. I'm certain she will come around."

"You think? She doesn't even look at me these days, Carrie."

"She's hurt," Carrie answered. "It's difficult to look at people that hurt you. And honestly, some of this is my fault."

'No." Peter shook his head. "It's mine. I should have told her."

Just as Carrie was about to respond, Amy walked out of the house and joined them on the porch. She glanced at Peter like she had formed a habit of doing in the last two weeks and took the bag from his hand.

"You made chicken soup?" she asked, keeping her head down.

"How'd you know?" Peter asked.

"I can smell it. It smells good. But you didn't have to. I was already planning on making something for lunch."

"I wanted to."

This was the longest conversation they had exchanged in two weeks. Perhaps, Jamison was right. Peter just needed to give Amy some time. While he was glad it was working, Peter hoped there were something he could do to speed up the process. He wanted his wife home with him.

"I miss you, Amy," Peter said gently. "It hurts that you won't even look at me."

Amy lifted her head, met his gaze for a second and then looked back down at the ground. "Are you staying for lunch?" she asked him.

"No. I have to get this second bag to Eugene's house. After that, I'm going home," Peter said.

"Oh, come on, Peter," Carrie said. "Stay for lunch."

"I didn't pack enough," he answered, smiling at Carrie. "I'll be back during dinner. Amy, would you like me to get you food from the diner we go to?"

"You don't have to," she replied.

"Do you want me to?"

"Yes, she does," Carrie responded in Amy's stead. "She does, Peter."

Peter nodded and stood upright. "I'll see you during dinner, Carrie. Bye, Amy."

There was no use waiting for her to respond. Amy wasn't going to. After giving her one last look, Peter made his way out of the yard. Making up with Amy was taking too long. But he had no choice but to wait. Peter held on to the hope that somehow, she would realize that his past didn't matter.

A while later, he arrived at Eugene's home and met Gloria seated on the short wooden steps just outside the house. She had her knees to her chest, and she stared into space.

"What are you thinking about, Mrs. Tompkins?" Peter asked, joining her. He sat by her side and set the bag down. "You're always thinking about something every time I come here to see Eugene."

Gloria scoffed. "I wasn't thinking. You brought chicken soup."

Peter's jaw dropped in surprise. "Let me guess. You can smell it?"

"I can," Gloria said, giggling.

"That's the exact same thing Amy said. It's strange," Peter voiced. "But yes, I did bring some soup for you and Eugene."

"Thank you, Peter," Gloria said to him. "You've been so kind to us ever since the incident. I can't thank you enough."

"It's the little I can do," Peter told her. "By the way, where is Eugene?"

"Sleeping," she answered. "Steven is with him too, sleeping. The boy refuses to leave Eugene's side even though I keep telling him that his father needs time to rest. Eugene doesn't mind, so I let it slide. But I would much rather prefer that Eugene rests without Steven stuck to his body."

Peter chuckled. "What you should be worried about is the fact that Steven loves his father now, more than he loves you."

Gloria fiddled with her fingers and smiled. "Cheeky, but it's good isn't it? I so wanted this to be good for both of us, I'm so happy that it is. If I think of all the things Eugene has done for Steven, I can understand why they love each other."

"Me too," Peter said and rose to his feet. "I should be on my way, Gloria. I'll be back tomorrow to check on Eugene."

"Wait, Peter. I need to talk to you," Gloria said. "Can you please sit?"

Hesitant at first, Peter sat back down by her side and interlocked his fingers. "What's wrong?"

"Nothing is wrong, there's just something we should have talked about a while ago," Gloria started. "It's about you and Amy. Now that I have some time to process the events of your wedding day, I have to ask where you and Amy stand. I heard what Mitch said that day, and I'm sorry for not jumping in to clear the air that instant. Eugene had been shot and I wasn't even thinking straight. What's going on? What did Amy say?"

Peter heaved a heavy sigh. "I'm scared Amy might end our marriage before it even starts, Gloria. She's hurt that I chose her as a second option because you and I didn't work out."

"Peter, you cannot let her think this way."

"I know," he said. "I'm trying, but she won't let it go. I don't know what to do at this point but wait for her to come around. But what if she just drifts further away from me while I wait for her? I truly love Amy, Gloria. I cannot lose her."

Gloria took her time to think. "Can you take the soup inside and watch the house until I return?"

Peter's forehead furrowed. "Why? Where are you going?"

"To see Amy," Gloria said. "I'm partially to blame for this too. I think I should talk to her."

Peter shook his head. "I don't think that will do a lot of good. Perhaps we should just..."

"Trust me," Gloria said, rising to her feet. "Wait here for me, and watch the house. I'll be back as soon as I talk to Amy, all right?"

Peter dropped his shoulders. "All right."

As Gloria hurried out of the house, Peter walked into the house. All he could do was hope that something good came out of Gloria interfering. The last thing he wanted was to make matters worse than they already were.

CHAPTER TWENTY-ONE

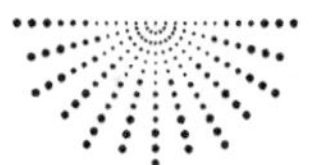

Amy sat on the bench on the porch where Carrie had previously sat. Carrie had taken the bag and the soup inside with her; it was such a sweet gesture that Peter had made. She was supposed to be living with Peter now, in their home. But Amy couldn't bring herself to go with him.

Peter had confessed that he missed her, and it took a lot of will for her not to say it back. Why did their situation have to be so complicated? Why wasn't Peter honest with her from the start? He never lied, but withholding the truth was lying too. How serious were his feelings for Gloria? How did he feel seeing her every day, knowing that he could have married someone so pretty, but that he had to settle for her because Gloria didn't want him?

Amy didn't know what to do. Was she over thinking it? Was she taking it too seriously?

"Amy?"

The sound of Gloria's voice startled her back to reality. Amy raised her head to find Gloria staring down at her. She had been so lost in thoughts that she hadn't heard her walk into the yard.

"Good morning, Gloria," Amy answered. "How are you? How is Eugene?"

When it came to Gloria, Amy had no idea how she was meant to feel. The lady had been nothing but kind to her, and she welcomed her with opened arms. But it still didn't change the fact that Gloria lied to her. Amy recalled sensing that Gloria was intentionally keeping things from her. Back then, she had thought that she was imagining things, but it turned out that she had been right to be suspicious.

"We're fine, thank you for asking," Gloria said and sat down. "Eugene is recovering."

"That's good news," Amy stated.

"How are you, Amy?"

Amy sighed and leaned back. "I'm fine too."

An awkward silence ensued. Amy had no idea what to say, given that Gloria was the one that approached her in the first place. She waited, hoping that Gloria would break the silence soon.

"Amy," Gloria started. "I know you feel hurt right now. I heard what Mitch Stokes said at your wedding. But must you let something that a criminal said mess with your head?"

"He wasn't wrong, Gloria," Amy said quietly. "The way he said it was rather harsh, but he wasn't wrong."

"Yes, he was."

"Why didn't you tell me?" Amy asked, turning to face Gloria. "Why did you keep it from me?"

"Because of something like this," Gloria responded. "Amy, whatever Peter and I had in the past doesn't matter at all. We tried, and we failed. Did you really not expect him to try and find a match for himself? He won't stay alone forever just because he and I couldn't find any common ground, just because we weren't in love."

"No one is faulting him for moving on," Amy said. "But we both know that if you and Peter got married, I would not be here."

"But we didn't," Gloria replied. "Amy, Peter wants a family. He wants children of his own that will fill his house with laughter because he was lonely growing up. I couldn't give him any children even if I wanted to. Besides, I didn't plan to fall in love with Eugene instead, but that happened and it became the turning point."

"But doesn't this mean that marrying me was a means to an end?" Amy questioned. "If you could have given Peter children, he would not have sent for me. Did he not go back to Carrie and ask her for a childbearing woman instead? Wasn't this the goal for him? I always wondered why he didn't have a problem with my appearance."

Gloria sighed. "Is that what's bothering you, Amy? You think Peter settled for you because he wants children, and you can give him that?"

Amy looked away, fighting back the tears in her eyes. "It's the truth, is it not? I am just a replacement, an ugly woman. I didn't want to marry like this, Gloria. I wanted a man that would marry me because he loved me genuinely, not because I could give him what he wants. What about me?"

"Don't say that you aren't beautiful, with such a wonderful smile. Deep down, you know that isn't true,

Amy," Gloria said. "You know. I understand you, and I understand why you would be hurt by this. Forgive me for not telling you, but I didn't think it mattered. There was nothing between me and Peter. Don't let the words of a man that nearly beat your husband half to death bother you so much."

Amy sniffed. "What do you mean?"

Gloria took Amy's hand. "You recall Drusilla telling you that she had to care for Peter when she first arrived?"

Amy nodded.

"Well, it was Albie, Mitch, and some other men that almost killed Peter because they wanted to rob him," Gloria said. "Now, Peter is one of the reasons the gang were stopped. Don't you think Mitch would have wanted to spite him? It's really not how it seems at all. Peter and I never loved each other and we understood this. That's why we are able to stay friends. He was never happy with me. In fact, I had never seen him smile so brightly like he did on his wedding day. I know Peter, and you know him too. Do you really think he would have married you if he didn't love you? As much as he wants children, love is important to him too. Did he not tell you this?"

Peter had mentioned it before, but Amy had been too hurt to take his word for it. Perhaps, she was overreacting. They were already married, and that wasn't going to change. Amy loved Peter, but the fear that he didn't love her too still lingered.

"Talk to him," Gloria said. "Peter has been lonely for a long time. Now, he is excited that he is married to you, but as the days go by, he fears you want to end the marriage. You have every right to be hurt, but talk to him and see if you can arrive at an understanding. Deep down, you know Peter loves you, for you."

"You must think I'm crazy," Amy mumbled. "I know this, but I can't face him without feeling sorry for him and for me."

Gloria sighed. "I need you to have a conversation with your husband, Amy. I have been married before, and let me tell you... being in a loveless marriage is worse than being single. From the start, it was about love for Peter. He married you because of this, trust me. He doesn't see you as a child bearer, or a means to an end, he sees you as the love of his life, as his soul mate. Will you just talk to him?"

Amy fiddled with her fingers. "I'll talk to him. Thank you, Gloria."

"There's no need to thank me," Gloria answered. "I apologize again for intentionally keeping the information away from you. Perhaps, if we had told you about it, then Mitch's words wouldn't have this great of an effect on you. I truly didn't keep it from you with bad intentions."

"I can see why you did it," Amy said and shrugged her shoulders. "I understand it was with good intent, I just can't help how I feel."

Gloria patted Amy on the back. "Talking to Peter will clear that up for you."

Amy hoped so, for she loved Peter, but could she ever trust him?

CHAPTER TWENTY-TWO

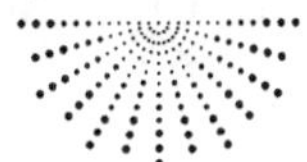

It felt as though some of the weight on Amy's chest had been lifted after her conversation with Gloria. She still sat on the porch, enjoying the cool breeze on her skin, as she thought about all that Gloria had said.

Drusilla and the baby were asleep, Jamison had gone to the mine to fill in for Eugene and Peter, and Carrie was in the living room. Amy shut her eyes as she sank deeper into her thoughts. She had about an hour or two to spare before the baby woke up again.

Jamison and Drusilla had named the little girl Carolyn. A shorter way to call it would be Carrie, just like how they called little Carolyn's grandmother. It had been

Drusilla's idea to name the girl after Carrie to honor all the efforts the lady had put into their lives.

"You're still here, Amy," Carrie noted, limping over to the bench. "You've been by yourself all day today. Well, you've been by yourself for a while, but you've been awfully quiet today."

"I'm just thinking," Amy mumbled.

"Do you mind sharing what it's about with me? Sooner or later, you will have to talk to me about this, you know?"

"How could you offer me to a man that once wanted somebody else, Carrie?" Amy asked, staring blankly into the yard. "Why did you tell me that Peter was excited to find a bride when all he wanted was someone to fill Gloria's place?"

Carrie remained silent for a minute and then sighed. "The match with Gloria was wrong from the start, Amy. It was never about finding someone to fill Gloria's place. It was about finding Peter his match. You're not a replacement, my dear."

Amy turned to Carrie. "But why does it feel like I am? I really don't want to feel like this, but I can't help it. You should have been honest with me from the start."

"Amy" – Carrie reached for her chin and pinched it. "You're overthinking this. Right from the start when Gloria arrived here in the town, she was tilting towards Eugene. I know she came here to marry Peter, but she didn't fall in love with Peter, neither did he fall in love with her. It was something that would never have happened. Peter didn't leave Gloria because she rejected him. They both decided to find their happiness somewhere else. He asked me to find him someone that would be his bride. Someone that had things in common with him. You both like the same things, and you envision the same kind of family. Peter wanted you, Amy, he didn't settle for you because Gloria was unavailable. Why would you choose to believe anything else?"

"Look at me, Carrie," Amy said. "And look at Peter. He's good looking, he is nice, and charming. I'm..."

"And so are you," Carrie cut her off. "You're a beautiful lady, Amy, and you should not think less of yourself. You're not ordinary like you claim to be. An ordinary person could not survive what you survived. Could not live through what you did."

"Oh, you're just saying that," Amy said, looking away.

"Peter loves you for you, Amy. Not for what you can give him," Carrie continued. "From the start, he was already invested in you. He shielded you from bullets with his body at the wedding, and the way he was smiling that day when you walked down the aisle completely caught me off guard. I've never seen him like that. Peter had never smiled so brightly before."

Carrie was the third person to tell Amy this. First, it was Drusilla, then Gloria, and now Carrie. Amy was starting to believe them. They all had known Peter longer than she had. Surely, they'd notice a change in his smile.

"How about you talk to Peter?" Carrie asked her. "It's only when you've talked to him that you'd know for sure what you want. It's been two weeks since the wedding. It's not normal that you're not be home with him. One thing Peter doesn't like is the feeling of loneliness. I thought that with you around, he didn't have to worry about it any longer."

"I know, but..."

"I understand, Amy. It's not your fault, it's ours. We should have told you, and you have every right to be angry. But don't punish Peter. It wasn't his intention to hurt your feelings."

"I'll talk to him," Amy said. "I don't know why it's now difficult for me to do so, but I'll talk to him."

"You're scared that if you talk to him, that things won't work out the way you want them to," Carrie said. "You know you want this to work. And Peter wants it to work too. So, for that to happen, you both need to come to an understanding. Come now, give me a hug if you forgive me."

Amy smiled faintly, and embraced Carrie. It was true that she really wanted things to work. But nothing was ever going to be the same if she kept feeling this way.

CHAPTER TWENTY-THREE

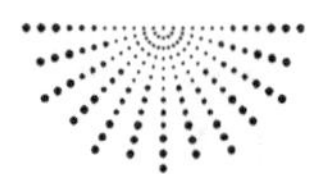

Amy stood by the fence, making sure to take deep breaths. Peter had asked to speak to her immediately after he arrived at the McCord house. It was good that way, seeing as she had imagined that he'd refuse to talk to her since she was avoiding him. But it was finally time for the conversation she had been avoiding.

Amy listened to Peter's footsteps as they approached her. He stopped a few feet away, and it took every will in her body to prevent her from turning around. Instead, she waited, hoping that he would start the conversation.

A few seconds later, she felt Peter's hand on her shoulder. Amy had no choice but to turn around, and when her eyes met Peter's, something softened inside of her. It was almost as if she had forgotten why she was angry in the first place.

Peter proceeded to take her hand into his and he stroked her wedding ring. "You're still wearing it. That's a good sign, I think. It means there's still hope for the both of us."

Amy pulled her hand away from his and turned to stare out over the fence. "I don't know, Peter. But we're married, and that's not going to change, so, of course, I'm wearing my wedding ring."

"Is that the only reason you're wearing your ring, Amy?" Peter asked her. "You really don't think there's hope for us?"

"Peter, that's not the point," Amy said, turning to him. "Don't do that. Don't try to sweet talk your way out of this. It won't work."

"I don't know what to do," Peter said with a quaking voice. "I don't know what else to say to you. Why won't you trust me?"

"Why won't you come clean and just admit that I am only here in Colorado to fulfil the desires that Gloria couldn't give you?"

"I cannot admit something that isn't true," Peter said clearly. "I will not admit to it, Amy. I will not say what you want to hear, because it's not the truth I know. It might seem so obvious, but it was not my intention. Don't put words into my mouth."

Something about Peter getting defensive caused Amy to mellow. She swallowed hard and crossed her arms, hoping that he did not sense the change in her demeanor.

"Will you just listen to me?" Peter asked.

"I'm listening," Amy mumbled.

"I mean, will you listen to me without arguing my point like it's a debate?" Peter questioned. "I need you to listen and to understand me, Amy. Not listen to respond."

Amy inhaled deeply and dropped her hands to her side. "I'm listening," she said, louder than before.

"Thank you," Peter whispered. "But first..."

Before Amy could react, Peter came in for a hug. He embraced her, clamping his body over hers and letting his hands pat her back like she was a child.

"What are you doing?" Amy asked with a muffled voice.

"We've been married for two weeks, and in that space of time you have deprived me of your touch," Peter answered. "Just give me one minute, and we'll get back to our discussion."

Amy clenched her fingers into a fist to stop herself from hugging him back. Instead, she shut her eyes, and basked in the warmth of the moment. A tiny voice in her head questioned her decisions. *Why was she being so stubborn? Was her argument worth depriving herself of Peter's warm embrace?* She felt so safe in his arms, why didn't she let this go? Perhaps, she could just let go of everything and give in to the moment.

Right when Amy lifted her hands to return the hug, Peter let go of her and took a step back.

"All right, let's do this now, shall we?" he said and cleared his throat. "I'm not leaving here until we come to a solution. That's why I want you to listen, so we can be logical about this."

Amy crossed her arms.

"I admit to the fact that I wanted to marry Gloria at first," Peter started. "Gloria and I courted with the intention of marriage in the near future. But I always wanted one thing, and that's a marriage of love; well, two things, and one filled with children. Gloria revealed to me after weeks of courting that she couldn't give me children and she felt guilty knowing that she was leading me on when she knew what I really wanted."

Amy sighed and was about to say something when Peter cupped her face with his hands, catching her off-guard.

"That wasn't the reason we didn't marry in the end," Peter continued. "I know what you were about to say. Even though Gloria said that to me, I still wanted to marry her because I felt responsible for her since she came to Gray Rock for me. I held Gloria in high-regard and I cared for her and Steven, but I wasn't in love with her. So, my plan had been to settle for a loveless marriage. But at the time, Gloria was already in love with someone else. Eugene. One of us had found love. She did, I did not. So, we talked about it, and I made a promise to her and myself that I would not settle for anything less than what I wanted. A marriage of love. You're here today, as my wife, Amy, because I chose not to settle. I chose to actively find someone that I could fall in love with. Someone that shared my interests, my likes. You're not here to replace Gloria. You are here because I was searching for love. One like Jamison and Drusilla had, one like Eugene and Gloria's love. Love brought you here, not my need for children. If children were really all I was after, do you really think I would have waited seven months until I found the perfect one for me?"

Amy placed her hand on Peter's arm and pulled it away from her cheek. "Peter, why didn't you..."

"Tell you from the start?" Peter asked. "Honestly, Amy, if I knew that you would react in this manner, I would have taken it to my grave. But the reason I didn't say anything was because I didn't think it was that important. Eugene and Gloria are in their own world right now. Jamison and Drusilla too. I started to feel that world with you, and then nothing else mattered. I don't want you thinking like this, Amy. It breaks my heart."

"Can you blame me?" Amy asked, close to tears. "You were my first everything. I have never kissed anybody else. I came this far for my first relationship, hoping it would be my last. But I got so jealous knowing... or thinking that you have loved someone else and you were forced to settle for me. I'm not the prettiest lady, and I'm not special. There's Gloria who is..."

"Gloria is Gloria, Amy," Peter cut in. "You are Amy Quinn, the most beautiful woman I have ever seen. I would never betray myself by settling for someone that will not make me happy. I was close to doing that with

Gloria, but... thank the heavens, I am glad I did not. Amy, you are the smartest woman I have met, your smile is so charming that I see it in my sleep, there's this thing you do with your glasses when they fall down to the bridge of your nose and you have to..."

Instinctively, Amy reached for her glasses with her finger and pushed them forward to sit on her face better. She instantly chuckled, noticing that she had done the exact thing Peter was just about to say.

Peter chuckled too, as he stroked her cheek. "I don't want to lose you, Amy," he said and sighed. "There is so much we can achieve together. We can learn from each other, and share stories about our similar past. We can raise children together, and teach them about the world. You have introduced me to what love is. I told Carrie when she showed me your letters. I told her I did not want to go through another mismatch. Carrie assured me that I'd be glad I met you. She was right. So, can you please give us another chance, Amy? Give me a chance to prove it to you. Right now, you don't have to forgive me. All I ask is that you let me prove my love to you."

Amy dropped her head and took off her glasses. "I don't know what the future holds, but what I am certain of, is the fact that I really want this to work too. I didn't know what to expect coming here to this faraway part of the country. But I recall how happy I was walking down the aisle. I want to go back to feeling like that, Peter."

"I will do my best to make sure that you do," Peter said. "Can you trust me to try, Amy?"

Amy inhaled sharply and responded with a firm nod. "I'm sorry if I hurt you with my silence."

Peter placed a kiss on her forehead and gathered her into his arms.

"You have nothing to apologize for, Mrs. Quinn."

Amy smiled, feeling warm tingles in her stomach at the sound of her new name. It was the first time he had called her that, and she realized how satisfying it felt to hear. How much it made her heart sing.

CHAPTER TWENTY-FOUR

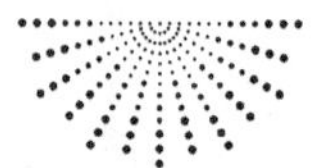

The bed creaked when Amy turned to her side. It was her second night in her new home, and so far, the awkwardness had not left. Amy had not thought about it, but living with Peter wasn't how she imagined it to be. They were comfortable around each other, no doubt, but there were times during the night, when they both retreated to their room, that Amy felt so tense, her palms started to sweat. This was a man she knew, and got married to. Why was she nervous to be alone with him all of a sudden?

The night before, Amy had fallen asleep before Peter got home, hence, it wasn't as awkward. Peter had gone to see Eugene, and he ended up spending more time than he had said he would. After waiting up nervously for Peter for over an hour, Amy didn't realize it when she fell asleep. She only noticed that Peter was by her side in the middle of the night when she touched him as she stretched.

Once she was awake, Amy spent a long time watching Peter sleep, and smiling to herself. It was a weird thing to do, but she couldn't help it. There were intervals where she would giggle and run her finger over his hair.

Now, on the second night they were spending together after she moved in, Peter was still awake. Amy hoped that he would fall asleep soon so she could admire him again like she had done the night before, but even with her back turned to him, she could tell he hadn't slept yet.

"Are you asleep?" Peter asked with a husky voice.

Amy turned around and faced him. "Not yet," she answered. "I can't sleep."

"If I fall asleep, will you play with my hair again like you did last night?" he asked.

Amy gasped at his question and lifted her head. "You were awake?"

"I wasn't at first," Peter said, chuckling. "But I heard you laughing, and I woke up. Then, you started playing with my hair, and I just laid there until you got tired and fell asleep."

"Why didn't you say something?"

"It seemed like you were having fun," Peter answered. He placed his arm around her and guided Amy to his body.

Amy sank into his embrace, listening to the rhythm of his heartbeat. "I was nervous. I still am, but... I don't understand it."

"I'm nervous too," Peter said, caressing her hair. "But I reckon it's because we are still trying to get used to this. Would you feel better if I arranged the guest room for you to use in the meantime?"

"No." Amy shook her head. "I'd rather be here, nervous and all. We're married after all, and this feels nice."

"All right then," Peter said.

Amy placed her chin on Peter's chest and stared at him. "Do you recall our first meeting? When you came to fetch me from the stagecoach."

"Of course, I do."

"When I first saw you, I was dazed. I even forgot what breathing was," Amy confessed.

Peter scoffed. "No, you weren't."

"I was," she answered. "I saw this tall, very handsome man, and for a minute I was not sure you were Peter Quinn. Then you introduced yourself, and you smiled... and from that moment I was swooning over you."

Even without seeing Peter's face, Amy could tell he was smiling.

"It was the same for me," Peter said.

"Oh, you don't need to lie to make me feel better."

"What?" Peter voiced, sitting up. "I'm being honest."

"I understand that you might have liked me later on, but that very moment when you saw me, you didn't think of me as pretty, did you? Of course, you didn't."

"Wait a minute. Don't answer the question for me," Peter said.

"I called you handsome, and you responded by asking if I was hungry," Amy argued.

"That wasn't my response," Peter said. "I asked the men for tips before I came to get you, and Lenard told me never to make a comment about your appearance. He said ladies didn't like that."

"What lady doesn't like to be called pretty?"

"I didn't want to..." Peter groaned. "I didn't even realize. I admit that when I saw you, I had no comment to give. I was just happy you had arrived. But then, you were so excited to see me, you smiled and you instantly stole my heart. Have you seen your smile, Amy? It can wake a dead man from the grave."

Amy threw her head back laughing. "Oh, Peter."

"I'm serious. No one has been that excited to see me before. But the way you looked at me, like you knew me already. Then you proceeded to study me and figure out that I was telling a lie only five minutes into our meeting. Come on. The connection was there from the start. This was meant to be."

Amy smiled and leaned on Peter. "I think so too."

They laid back on the bed, embracing each other. Amy smiled, and let herself get in tune with the rhythm of Peter's heartbeat. Saying she was content with her life in that moment was an understatement. Amy had found happiness.

EPILOGUE

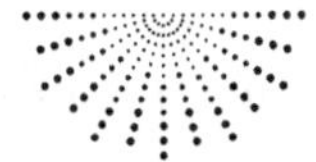

The famous weekly dinner.

Even after Jamison and Drusilla had moved into their new home, close to Carrie's property, Carrie still hosted all of them for dinner once a week. Carrie now lived alone, but she was almost never at home alone. It was either she paid Drusilla and the baby a visit, or she came over to Amy's home to spend the day.

Amy recalled how dramatic Carrie had been when Jamison and Drusilla moved out of the home. She had asked them not to, and told them that it was unfair of them to leave her all alone. Her reaction puzzled Amy, because Carrie had been present from the time Jamison and Drusilla began building their own home, until the time it was completed. Yet, she still tried to get them to stay with her.

But over time, Carrie got used to not having anyone around her home. She was proud of all of them and she made it very clear. Little Carolyn was her pride and joy. She would show her off to everyone whenever she got the chance. Strangely, seeing Carrie happy filled Amy with joy. The woman was responsible for her new life after all.

"Amy, darling. Please set the table while I finish up here in the kitchen," Carrie told her.

Amy set the plates down on the dining table, making sure that the cutlery was set up around each plate. Eugene had made a full recovery. Although after six months, he still couldn't move his shoulders as high as he could before. The doctor had informed them that it was a slow process, and that they should give it time. It was still going to take about a couple of months before Eugene's shoulder was back to normal, but he was already set to return to the mines. He claimed that he had been away for too long.

Gloria was now a good friend of Amy's. They had formed an understanding, and Amy loved the times they spent with Drusilla, gossiping about their husbands. They could go on and on for hours, giggling. The three of them saw each other every day. They would sometimes exchange meals, or even cooked together. When they had started the practice five months ago, it had been difficult for Amy to participate. She wasn't used to it, and she always found it hard to say the right words. But over time, as she got more and more comfortable, now, speaking to Drusilla and Gloria was easy.

"We're here!" Jamison announced, walking into the house with Drusilla and Carolyn. "What smells so delicious?"

"Welcome," Amy beamed.

The first person Amy said hello to was Carolyn. She took the little girl in her arms and cooed. Carolyn had inherited Drusilla's eyes, and that was it. The rest of her features were gotten from Jamison. Her pointed nose, round face, and blonde hair. Jamison always bragged about how Carolyn was his twin. Sometimes it was apparent he said it just to rub off on Drusilla, and it always worked.

"Hello, Amy. The turkey smells wonderful," Drusilla complimented, taking her seat at the table. "I'm starving."

"Well, Carrie made the turkey, so the compliment should go to her," Amy said, sitting by Drusilla's side. "But I helped. A little. You know how Carrie likes to cook. There's not much you can do when she takes charge of the kitchen."

"That is true," Drusilla noted.

"We have arrived," Eugene announced.

"We have arrived," Steven repeated, following behind Eugene.

Amy rose to her feet and greeted Gloria with a hug. The ladies exchanged pleasantries and sat down.

"You are glowing, Mrs. Tompkins," Drusilla said.

"Am I?" Gloria asked, touching her face. "I don't feel like I am. Steven is going through a phase where he repeats everything Eugene says, and it's frustrating trying to get him to quit it."

"Oh, just let him," Amy said. "It's cute."

"It was cute. Now, I'd really like him to stop," Gloria said with a sigh. "Enough about me. How are you doing? Let me say hello to little Carolyn."

Amy carefully handed Carolyn over to Gloria. "I'll be right back. I need to help Carrie in the kitchen."

When most of them arrived, they all gathered in the living room and talked. Dinner couldn't start without Peter, and he wasn't back from the mines yet. After Eugene's accident, Peter had taken on a major role at the mine. Jamison wasn't much help in that aspect, as he had a new born to take care of, and a recovering wife. However, now that Eugene had declared his intentions to return to the mine, Peter's workload was going to reduce. Thankfully.

"Any news about Albie's gang?" Jamison asked Eugene. "Do you think we should ask the sheriff to station men at the outskirts of the town, just in case?"

"There's no need for that," Eugene answered. "Albie's gang is done. I confirmed that the sheriff captured all of them, and they are now behind bars. We've heard the last of them."

"That's a relief," Carrie said. "I won't ever forgive them for ruining Amy's wedding day."

"That day still feels unreal," Drusilla chimed in. "I can't believe I was able to give birth to Carolyn in such a state. I was scared for my life, and for hers at the same time."

Jamison took her hand and interlocked their fingers. "We made it through. That's what matters."

"I'll never forget the look on Jamison's face when my water broke," Drusilla said, laughing. "He looked ashen white, like he had seen a ghost or something. It took him a rather long time to process all that was happening."

"I honestly don't know how I was able to keep myself together that day," Jamison said. "It was a miracle, really."

Amy listened to them discuss the incident, and what they could have done differently. In that moment, she realized that there was no place she'd rather be. Virginia had been tolerable because of Percival, her good friend, and her children, but Gray Rock was home. People in the town all knew and loved each other. With the bandits gone, Amy could peacefully walk the streets of the town at night, with Peter by her side. They had come to love taking strolls. Amy had come to love everything about the town.

"What are you thinking about, Amy?" Carrie asked, noticing that she was silent.

Amy sat up and a soft smile formed on her lips. "Everything. You. This family. It's nice."

"I said the same thing when I got married to Jamison," Drusilla noted. "It's nice, isn't it?"

"I've never been close with this many people before," Amy revealed. "I've never known this many people. But here, I didn't just find friends, I got a family. I don't know how to explain it, but thinking about it keeps me up, daydreaming at night. You won't understand how good it feels."

"I understand," Drusilla and Gloria chorused.

The three of them exchanged looks and giggled. They communicated with their eyes, thankful that they had found one other. They were living their best lives, knowing that they had each other's backs.

Jamison pulled Drusilla into his embrace and rubbed her arms. "You three speak as if it was one sided. Mother, will you please remind Drusilla the kind of man I was before she entered my life?"

"And will you please tell Gloria the kind of man I was before I decided to find a bride?" Eugene chimed in.

Carrie chuckled. "With pleasure. Drusilla... Gloria, I want to be selfish and thank you both for responding to my letters. When I began hassling Jamison to find a wife, it was for one reason. I didn't want him to be alone when I passed on. You see, before Drusilla, Jamison never even glanced at a woman. He always said it wasn't time, and that when the time came, he'd know. This worried me. So, I took matters into my own hands. Now, thinking about it, I don't want to pass on so quickly after seeing the result of my well thought out decision. I feel proud of myself hearing you all confess your feelings to each other. It brings me to the brink of tears every time."

"Oh, Carrie," Drusilla said. "Thank you for writing to me. I really needed you that time in my life. It's almost as if you were sent to me."

"I feel the same way too," Gloria said. "I never thought I would fall in love again. I had tried marriage once... a loveless one, and I thought love wasn't possible for me anymore. But look at me now. Happy. Content."

"I think I speak on behalf of Eugene, Peter and I when I say we feel the exact same way," Jamison said. "When people claim that love changed them, I always laugh. My mother for one always said that marrying my late father changed her life. She always told me it would be the same for me but I never took her word for it. Until, I experienced the power of love myself."

"When did you realize you were in love with Drusilla, Jamison?" Amy asked him.

Jamison tilted his head to the side, thinking. "When I saw her in danger, and I was ready to rip grown men in half."

"That says a lot because Jamie is a peaceful person," Eugene noted.

"What about you, Eugene?" Amy asked him.

"Well, it's almost the same for me. I saw Gloria in danger, and I confessed my feelings for her to Peter by accident. I wanted to keep it a secret because Gloria had been promised to Peter, but hearing that she had been taken... I couldn't keep it inside me anymore."

"Would you like me to tell you the moment we knew Peter was in love with you?" Jamison asked Amy.

Amy felt the heat rise in her cheek because she already knew the answer. "When he shielded me from bullets with his body?"

Jamison sucked in his teeth. "Well, that was confirmation, but the real moment was when he left work at the mine to go buy you lilies because he had just recalled that you liked flowers."

"He left in the middle of working," Eugene added. "That's very unlike Peter. Usually, he finishes his work before he even eats."

Amy smiled sheepishly as she fiddled with her fingers. They didn't need to tell her how much Peter loved her. He showed it to her every day with his actions. Sometimes, Amy wondered if he would ever get tired of it.

"I've arrived! Where's my wife?"

The sound of Peter's voice caused Amy to shriek in excitement.

"Here! She's here!" Amy beamed, blushing.

Amy felt bloated and weak from the heavy dinner. They had to wait to have dessert, and bring the dinner to an end, so instead of sitting in the living room, Peter took her out for a walk.

They took their favorite route, holding hands and occasionally bumping into each other playfully. Amy had not thought she could love Peter any more than she did on her wedding day, but as the days went by, she proved herself wrong time and time again.

"You're staring at me," Peter said, keeping his eyes on the path.

"Am I not allowed to stare at my husband?" Amy blushed.

Peter chuckled lightly and placed a kiss on her forehead. "I'm sorry I was late to dinner today. There was an issue at the mine, and I had to stay until..."

"You don't have to apologize for working, Peter. I understand," Amy said to him. "You're doing a good thing covering for your friend at work. You should be proud."

"I just don't want you to have any... thoughts," Peter explained. "I know it's been six months, but I am still not sure you've forgiven me, and I wouldn't want to give you a reason to doubt my love for you."

Amy reciprocated his kiss by placing one of her own on his cheek. "I have known nothing but love as of late. I feel stupid for doubting you earlier. You have shown me what love really is, and I won't trade it for the world."

Peter stopped in his tracks. "You really meant that?"

"From the bottom of my heart," Amy answered without hesitation. "You not only gave me love, Peter. You gave me friends and family too. You know about my past, and you know how I lived. The one thing I always prayed for was a big family of my own. But we haven't even achieved this dream, and I already feel like part of the one I always prayed for."

Peter placed both hands on Amy's shoulders. "You have no idea how happy it makes me to hear you say this."

"I love you, Peter," Amy said. "I know this sounds weird, but I'm thankful that you and Gloria didn't match. I'm thankful that I was brought here to be by your side. The love I receive from you, and our family is so overwhelming that it's impossible not to reciprocate it."

Peter wrapped his hands around Amy, unable to contain his excitement. "I'll always do right by you. I promise. You are the most beautiful woman I have ever known. There's no one in this world I'd rather be with."

Amy had heard Peter call her beautiful to her face, and to other people so many times that she had accepted it to be the truth. There was also the manner in which he stared at her too whenever he watched her speak. Sometimes, it caused her words to get caught in her throat, and other times, Amy would just stare back at him, grinning. To think that she could have lost Peter because of her doubts caused Amy to shudder.

"I have news," Amy said and lifted her head to Peter's ear. "How does a new addition to our family sound? A little, cute addition that will be delivered to us in around seven and a half months?"

Peter gasped and broke the hug. "Are you saying..."

"Yes." Amy giggled. "That's exactly what I'm saying. Oh, it was so difficult to keep it a secret from the others."

"When – how?" he stuttered, beaming.

"I found out this afternoon when I went to see the doctor. I had suspected it for a while, but I needed to confirm it before telling you, and I did. I confirmed it, Peter. It's happening."

"Our very first baby?"

"Yes." Amy nodded.

Peter swept her up from the ground and spun her around. He showered Amy with so many kisses, she was unable to breathe.

"We must start making preparations," Peter said excitedly. "The crib, the baby's clothes... we must also get to know the midwife. She needs to tell us what we should and should not be doing. Or perhaps, we should just ask Carrie or Drusilla or Gloria? They should know. All right, we'll ask them, and then we'll still get the midwife."

Amy giggled. "First we have to tell them."

"Right," Peter said and clapped. "We have to make the announcement. It's perfect."

"How about we tell them right after we have dessert?"

"Whatever you say," Peter answered and hugged Amy again. "Oh, Amy. I am so happy. Where have you been all my life?"

Amy shut her eyes and tightened her arms around Peter. "We're together now, that's what matters."

"Amy," Peter said softly. "You know your happiness is what truly matters to me, more than anything."

Amy was certain of the fact that there would be nothing but better days ahead of them. Their first child was going to be the start of something magical. A family they both wanted more than anything.

Amy smiled to herself, excited about the future that was about to unfold. "I know and I love you. I feel so lucky to be your bride." She kissed him and melted into his arms, the safest place to be.

"No, my love, I am the lucky one," he said against her lips before he kissed her once more.

If you missed book 1 The Miners Courageous Bride you can grab it here or read on for a fabulous bargain.

Amazing Box Set of sweet romances FREE with KU or just 0.99 for a limited time.

Bradley jolted awake, his heart pounding as a sudden screaming filled the room. It crushed his heart and made his head feel like it was about to explode. Dragging himself out of his sleep, Bradley rolled over and looked at the crib by his bed. His daughter was lying there, trying to chew on her blanket as she screamed, tears rolling down her chubby red cheeks.

Not again. This was the third time this week Charlotte had woken up in the middle of the night. Normally, she slept pretty well, but lately, she had been really struggling. Bradley had no idea what was wrong with her and it chewed up his insides hearing it. It made him feel inadequate. Whatever it was, it left Charlotte in a lot of pain, judging by the cries.

Sighing, Bradley rubbed his eyes and sat up, leaning over the side of the crib.

"What's the matter now, sweetie? Come here."

Charlotte clung to him as Bradley lifted her, cuddling her against his chest as he sat on the edge of the bed, rocking her gently while he stroked her head. For a moment, he was struck by how heavy his daughter was getting. It only seemed a moment ago that she was so light he was afraid of dropping her in case she broke into many pieces. She had been tiny, and she didn't wriggle as much. Bradley had stared at her for hours, wondering how he was a father to such a beautiful child.

If only Jacqueline was around to see her daughter grow. A pang of grief hit him, whenever he looked at Charlotte. His daughter was the spitting image of her mother, and Bradley felt the hollow sensation in his chest getting bigger each time. Jacqueline was supposed to be here, raising their child together. She shouldn't have been taken like that.

The pain of her death was getting easier to deal with, but not by much. Bradley had work and his daughter to focus on. Charlotte more than anything eased the pain. She needed his time, money, attention, and love, and Bradley had made himself a promise not to let his daughter go without. Caring for her prevented him from wallowing in his own self-pity.

She was still crying in his arms, now chewing on his fingers. Perhaps she was hungry. Putting her on the bed for a moment, Bradley tugged on his trousers, shrugging on a shirt but not buttoning it up. Charlotte whined more as he dressed, it quietened a little when he picked her up again.

"Come on, you. Let's go outside and have a walk around the garden."

Maybe some fresh air would help. It had worked wonders when Charlotte was a newborn and just wouldn't sleep, even after being nursed. Emma had suggested fresh air to help, and it had. So much so it had left Bradley feeling sleepy.

As he went downstairs and out into the garden, Bradley found himself having more admiration for mothers. They did most of the work when raising children. They had to nurse the baby, get up with them in the night and entertain them. They were the ones who made sure their children were safe, fed, and well. Fathers did get involved, but it seemed natural to pass it all onto the mother. Bradley had more respect for mothers who did this with all their children, especially when there were lots of them. He didn't think he could cope with more than one child right now. Charlotte was more than enough.

Especially when he was alone.

Jacqueline shouldn't have died. She should be here now, helping him and giving Charlotte the cuddles she needed from a mother. But fate had got in the way, and she had died moments after giving birth. Bradley had held her in his arms as she slipped away, torn between relief that his daughter was alive and distraught that his wife was gone. The days after her death were a complete blur. If it hadn't been for Emma, Molly, and his neighbors, he would have gone down a different route.

Nine months later and Bradley still missed her. He was getting used to being the one who got up during the night when Charlotte needed something, and he was used to being exhausted going to work, but it didn't stop him from missing his wife.

He could only hope that Jacqueline would be proud of him.

Bradley walked once around the garden, and Charlotte did calm down a bit. She was still whining and chewing on her fingers, but she wasn't as loud as before. At least she wouldn't disrupt the neighbors at this time of night. Hopefully, he could get her back inside and nobody would have noticed.

Too late. There were footsteps, and then a head popped over the wall, searching the darkness as she raised a candle over her head.

"Bradley?"

"Oh, hey, Emma." Bradley grimaced, adjusting his hold on his daughter. "Sorry, I didn't mean to wake you."

"It's fine. I was awake, anyway."

"You are such a liar, Emma, do you know that?"

"Sorry. I hear a baby crying and I'm up." Emma Hilton gave him a sympathetic look. "Is she still not sleeping through?"

"No. I don't know why, either."

"Poor you." Emma started to climb down. "Go on back inside. Give me five minutes and I'll be over."

"There's no…"

"Don't be silly. I'm happy to help. Now off you go."

Bradley wasn't about to argue. Nobody argued with Emma Hilton, and he had to admit that she was the perfect neighbor for him in this situation. As a midwife, Emma knew how to look after a baby, especially one in distress. She had been a Godsend since Charlotte's birth, even looking after her while Bradley went to work. He had protested about it, but Emma argued that someone needed to earn for his family, and she was happy to help. She had even taken the little one to her job to be there whenever she was needed. Bradley had tried to pay her for it, and she refused.

He did feel like he was taking advantage of her, but Emma never complained. Then again, Emma was the type who was no-nonsense. She just went on with life without batting an eyelid. It didn't matter what happened, she was still going strong.

Heading into the house, Bradley took Charlotte into the living room and checked her over. She didn't need a change of diaper, and Charlotte refused anything to eat.

She just kept chewing her hand, and her cheeks seemed to have gotten red.

Bradley felt at a loss. What was wrong?

There was a knock at the door, and then Emma came into the room, a shawl over her gown with her long graying hair trailing down her back. She was carrying a damp cloth.

"What's that for?"

"I suspect that Charlotte might be teething. Her teeth are coming through and they can be very painful. A baby doesn't know what's going on." Emma sat on the couch and handed the cloth to Charlotte. "Let's see what she does with this."

Charlotte gave the cloth a cursory look before taking it. Bradley watched as she started sucking on the cloth. Her whines eased off, and then she was sucking away in silence. Her cheeks were still red, but she didn't look as distressed.

"Well, that actually worked."

Emma chuckled. "You didn't think it would?"

"I don't know. I felt like I was going mad." Bradley rubbed at his ears. "I think my head's still got a ringing noise."

"That's normal. You'll be fine soon." Emma stroked Charlotte's hair. "She's going to be fine, although you might have some broken sleep for a while."

"You mean no more than usual?"

"Fair point. You might be lucky and she sleeps for longer this morning."

Bradley grunted.

"And knowing my luck, I'll end up missing the start of my shift. Then I'll get unhappy people using the stagecoach."

"You'll be up. Don't worry about it." Emma patted his shoulder. "If you think being a parent to one is bad enough, try getting woken up in the middle of the night because someone's gone into labor and they're in a panic. I don't think I've slept properly since I was younger than you."

"Does it get better?"

"Of course, it does."

Bradley yawned. He loved his daughter, but he could feel his sleep suffering. That wasn't fair on Charlotte if he was complaining about lack of sleep, but Bradley didn't really want to fall off the coach when he was working because he was falling asleep. He had done that when he was wide awake, and the fall hadn't been pleasant. It was not something he wanted to go through again.

"What I really need is someone who does this full-time instead of me asking the neighbors for help. I think I could afford for someone to come in, but at the same time, I feel like I'm failing Charlotte by doing it."

"You mean get a nanny?"

"Is that the word? I'm too tired to think right now."

Emma smiled. "Well, I think it's a good idea. You're not going to fail Charlotte. You're making sure she's got someone with their full attention on her. It'll be worth the money."

"The problem is, the nannies in Lubbock are already in employment, and I don't think they would have time to take on another child."

"Then I might be able to help."

Bradley frowned. "How so?" Emma smiled and sat back.

"I have three young ladies coming to Lubbock tomorrow. You're picking them up from the next town."

"Young ladies?" It took a moment for Bradley's mind to clear. "These are the ladies you've brought in to find husbands?"

"Yes."

Emma, as well as being a midwife and helping Bradley, still wanted to do something. She was always trying to help others and women were in short supply. So, she decided to become a matchmaker. Bradley had laughed when she first said it, but Emma was determined. At first, though, there hadn't been anyone interested in coming to Texas to marry someone they hadn't met before. But, now three women were coming? Bradley wasn't sure whether to be impressed with Emma's tenacity or sorry for the women to be put in a position where they had to travel across the country for love that might not be there.

"Anyway, one of them said in her letters that she's a nanny in Chicago, and she would be looking for work once she got here. You could hire her to look after Charlotte."

"Hire her?" Bradley mused. "Would I be able to afford her?"

"More than likely. You won't know until you ask. It will certainly help you feel less stressed about raising Charlotte."

"And does that mean more sleep?"

Emma chuckled.

"Cheeky. It won't hurt to ask her, although maybe wait until she gets into Lubbock. She probably won't want to be accosted so suddenly."

Bradley yawned again, trying to hide it behind his hand. Charlotte was far calmer, snuggled up against his side as she chewed on the wet cloth. It seemed to be helping.

"I'm surprised you're even suggesting someone else, seeing as you love spending time with Charlotte. You could be a nanny yourself."

"I'm all for cuddling babies, but even I need my sleep."

"And you called me cheeky."

"At my age, I'm allowed." Emma yawned and got to her feet. "Speaking of sleep, I'd better go back. Will you be all right now?"

"I should be. Thanks, Emma."

"Any time." Emma leaned over and kissed his cheek. "Don't fret, Bradley. Things will work out... eventually."

Bradley hoped so. He really hoped so.

Grab this amazing box set - 26 Christmas Brides and Seasonal Wishes for FREE with Kindle Unlimited

The Brides of Broken Bow

If you missed any of this series, all three books are now available.
Each book covers one couple and is a complete story.

God bless,

Indiana Wake

Indiana Wake was born in Denver, Colorado, where she learned to love the outdoors and horses. At the age of eleven, her parents moved to the United Kingdom to follow her father's career.

It was a strange and foreign new world, and it took a while for her to settle down. Her mom raised horses and Indiana soon learned to ride. She would often escape on horseback imagining she was back in the Wild West. As well as horses, Indiana escaped into fiction and dreamed of all the friends she had left behind.

From an early age, she loved stories. They were always sweet and clean and, more often than not, included horses, cowboys, and most importantly of all a happy ever after. As she got older, she would often be found making up her own stories and would tell them to anyone who would listen.

As she grew up, she continued to write, but marriage and a job stole some of her dreams. Then one day she was discussing with a friend at church, how hard it was to get sweet and clean fiction. Though very shy about her writing Indiana agreed to share one of her stories. That friend loved the story and suggested she publish it on kindle. Together they worked really hard, and the rest, as they say, is history.

Indiana has had multiple number-one bestsellers and now makes her living from her writing. She believes she was truly blessed to be given this opportunity and thanks each and every one of her readers for making her dream come true.